FAMILIAR TIES
TALES OF MYTHON BOOK 2

KATHRYN JAYNE

Copyright (C) 2020 Kathryn Jayne

Layout design and Copyright (C) 2020 by Next Chapter

Published 2020 by Sanguine– A Next Chapter Imprint

Edited by Terry Hughes

Cover art by CoverMint

This book is a work of fiction. Names, characters, places, and incidents are the product of the author's imagination or are used fictitiously. Any resemblance to actual events, locales, or persons, living or dead, is purely coincidental.

All rights reserved. No part of this book may be reproduced or transmitted in any form or by any means, electronic or mechanical, including photocopying, recording, or by any information storage and retrieval system, without the author's permission.

TITLES BY KATHRYN JAYNE

Fiction:

Tales of Mython:
Salvation Kiss
Familiar Ties
Rekindled Sparks

Home is not a place of bricks and mortar, it is a feeling, one that can sometimes be found only in the arms of another.

PROLOGUE

There is no denying it. Hearing it is the year 224 can be quite confusing, especially if you don't know the real truth of history. But I am not talking B.C. or A.D. No, I am talking O.D. or Óla Dei, meaning 'all seen'. It's also, quite aptly, the abbreviation used for an overdose, which is something we all experienced a few hundred years ago, an overdose of the unseen. Our world forever changed, but you won't find that in your history books.

Before our year counter reset, your time ended, or at least it did for us. You continued on, unaware of what actually happened, and if my tales make it out of this region, then no doubt they will be passed over as fable, but this is our truth, this world is our truth.

As with most ends, it came as a complete force of devastation. The Doomsday clock leapt to midnight and the world as we knew it ended. But it wasn't missiles flying or chemicals assailing the sky, it was those who had existed unseen amongst us since the beginning, stepping into the light and making themselves known. These creatures, beings thought only to be spun from the minds of fablers like myself, had grown weary of living in the shadows, hiding their true nature, and Mankind fell to them in the blink of an eye and a new order was forced upon us.

But things changed too quickly, and the devastation was too great. That was when the Perennials came. Remember the story of how man obtained fire? Remember the gods of old? That was actually the Perennials. Invoking their powerful magics, these beings sacrificed themselves to rewrite history, turning back the clock for many minds and reaching into the great source of all to ensure no one your side would remember the truth.

They took it upon themselves to banish our land, remove it from sight and history, and seal within it as many of the creatures from your myths and legends as they could gather. Certain people in your history have worked alongside them, hunting these beings and directing their fate accordingly, sometimes relocating them to the island of Mython.

The problem is, Mython is a big island, and those of us here still have tales and books detailing the true history in all its horrific glory. Having seen how creatures had ravished the land, suffice to say our beginning was not an era of peace and harmony.

While the world outside had forgotten we had ever existed and moved into their new century, we eventually, through wars, rebellions and negotiations, found our own balance of sorts; one that is maintained by the most powerful of each race, those with Elder blood coursing through their veins.

Our country is divided into territories, each with its own elected leader who reports issues of note to the council, a collection of thirteen species predominately consisting of Elder bloodlines from the main preternatural lines such as shifter, fey, vampire, magical innate, elementals, celestials and so on. Humans were of course included, but we elect our own representatives just as any clan without such a sovereign did. The only missing faction is the Perennial, because none exist any more, at least none that we are aware of. After creating order, in our world and yours, it is said they invoked the last of their magic to seal our land from discovery.

Over two hundred years have passed since the wars died down and an uneasy truce was formed. The balance appears to be working. Now, life has returned to normal, or at least a manner of normal only possible here. Humans and preternatural are sharing space and resources, and the council are doing what is needed to maintain peace.

As I mentioned before, I am a fabler and it is my calling to tell the tales of our people. My name is Kathryn Jayne, and the tale here is just one of the many lives that call to me. Hopefully, what limited powers I have will guide it to your hands. Be it fiction in your eyes or not, these stories must be told.

CHAPTER 1

Don't look back, keep running. The mantra repeated in Jesse's mind as her bare feet tore across the stone walkway. Her brilliant white gown billowed around her while the crystal droppers in her honey-coloured hair shone like the morning dew in the sunlight. It was a beautiful day for a wedding, just so long as it wasn't hers.

She didn't think she would have had the chance to run. Her father had ensured she was barefoot, and the bone hoops embedded in the three tier petticoat sewn into her dress should have prevented her from escaping through the narrow window. But he had underestimated her resolve.

She half-skipped in pain, the soles of her feet already shredded from the rough, slightly damp stones of the path.

'How much further?' A sigh of relief escaped her lips as her bare soles connected with the smooth cobblestones of the elegant driveway, leaving faint prints of blood in her wake. She remembered this path, the way the horse-drawn carriage had vibrated on them as her father had warned her not to embarrass him any further than she already had.

The distant gatehouse beckoned. If she could just clear the driveway, she'd be free. She could lose them in the forest. A desperate breath wheezed in her chest, lungs burning from the effort. She wasn't used to such exertion, until today she had been all but a prisoner, locked in her room and visited only when her father's temper reigned.

She was a disappointment to him, a reminder of the woman he married, the woman he had killed with his own bare hands while her four-year-old self had stood and watched. She could never push that memory from her mind. She could still see the hatred in his eyes as he crushed the life from her while she struggled futilely. She'd never had a chance. But Jesse had one now, if she could just reach the forest.

'*No, this way,*' warned the tickle in her mind—her mother's madness, as her father called it. She looked for the reddish-tan coat of her caracal, Levi. His black tufted ears twitched, listening for any unseen threats. They were both aware that her absence been noticed and of the echoing sound of the heavy footsteps in pursuit. '*Quickly.*' There was a desperation to the thought, Levi needed her to escape as much as she did. He had been by her side for as long as she could remember, and he knew what she had endured.

Altering her path, she cried out as her slick feet slipped upon the cobblestones. Her hip screamed in agony as she landed hard, but she couldn't delay. Fighting with her billowing dress, she clawed herself to her feet, hurrying towards Levi. His spirit form was sitting in a large tree now, one whose thick boughs extended beyond the perimeter wall.

Bark embedded itself deep into her raw and bleeding feet as she scrambled up, her arms burning, chest heaving. She tugged at her dress, a slight feeling of satisfaction spurring her on as she heard the silken garment tear as she snatched it from the clutches of a broken branch.

A transparent arm reached down to her from above, extending through the bark of the tree as she struggled, while Levi warned that her pursuers were closing in.

'Take my hand.' Grasping for the spirit's hand, she watched in awe as her hand, along with the long lace sleeve of her gown, became invisible against the bark of the tree, its effect spreading down her limb, but not quickly enough.

"No, you don't," growled a deep voice as a thick arm encircled her waist, ripping her from the tree. She clutched on to the dryad's hand, kicking against the figure who dragged her back as her fingers were snatched away from salvation. Her chest heaved, the dark motes before her gaze growing until she felt her struggle cease as the world around her faded into darkness. Who was she kidding? She would never be free, and he was never coming back.

Alec sat on the train, staring through his brown-haired reflection, his honey-coloured eyes watching with growing discomfort as the scenery passed in a blur of greenery while fat raindrops bombarded his window.

The clatter of the wheels upon the track chuckled their mocking laughter, goading him as he made his way home. Home, the thought made him scoff. The last time he had thought of a place as being home, he had been a child, unaware of the fate awaiting him, of the life of servitude into which he had been born.

There was only one thing that had made his fate bearable, one person. Her letters had been a light in the darkness for the first four years of their separation, but in the last ten years not once had she written back to him. Not once. Without warning, her letters had simply stopped. He blew out a breath, lifting his thick, angular fringe slightly.

Despite her absence, he still found his gaze straying to the stars at night, seeking their constellations, wondering if she was doing the same. Even now, a sad smile tugged at his lips as he remembered nights huddled together in the garden, wrapped in blankets, while she invented their names and stories.

He never had the heart to correct her. Her tales were so much better.

What had happened to that girl? What became of Jesse, whose fair hair and blue eyes would cause even the most beautiful angel to pale in her presence, the girl he had known, from the moment her hand was placed in his, that home was not a place but the feeling he had when they were together. He missed those days as much as he still missed her. Things had been simpler then, and now she was married. She had moved on so easily, but he never had.

He remembered chasing her around the garden and listening as she spoke of magic and wonder and wove captivating tales of fairies and creatures who lived within the trees. The sound of her laughter had been enchanting, making a smile appear on the face of anyone who heard it. It wasn't a delicate sound like the tinkling of a bell, more like wind chimes trapped in a storm, full of passion and energy. Genuine. But her innocent laughter had never quite sounded the same after her mother had died.

When he entered his second septennial—the time when preternaturals' abilities gained strength—Lord Kyron had sent him away to be trained. That had been the second day he had seen bruises on her she wouldn't explain, the same kind of bruises he had seen on her mother. He still remembered his goodbye, a promise that he would return for her, that he would protect her. It was a vow he had broken many times over.

No wonder her letters had stopped, but if she'd read his surely she knew he was trying. Perhaps she hated him for leaving her there, for not trying hard enough to save her. For letting her down.

For fourteen years, he had been trained while working for her father. Fourteen years of being shaped for the duties he would be expected to fulfil and being mocked because he had been born without a shifter essence. Some said it was because he had been bound to the family too soon, that they should have waited for his other form to emerge first. He had been glad it was absent; he had seen how the animal side was beaten into submission since it was known the master's orders could control only the human. His inability to shift simply meant there was one less lesson to endure.

It had been a day before his seventh birthday when he had been forced to take the oath and be bound by blood and magic. He was their servant anyway, his line already bound, but this had been a necessary rite linking him to his master's will. At the time, it had seemed like nothing.

"—to further this, you will be acting in the capacity of bodyguard to Lord Kyron." Alec yawned as the old man before him droned on. His hooked nose reminded him of a vulture, an image not quite dispelled by his small beady eyes. The figure looked up disdainfully.

"No, please, do go on. I always yawn like this when I'm interested." Alec did not need to hear this again. He had spent years having the commitments and laws of his contract outlined and drilled into his mind.

He knew all about how his master could use their bond to draw his essence to him, and how the part of him summoned could be used as a shield reflecting any damage back to his own physical form. He understood all too well any order given was not a request but a compulsion that could not be refused.

The training had been to hone his skills, to ensure he had the best chance at protecting his master and surviving. Not once had he felt the compulsion of a command and he was certain he could overpower it. His mind was strong and, if he could break his family's curse, then perhaps he could even get Jesse to forgive him.

He wasn't sure why she had stopped writing to him, if he had put something that made her angry, hurt her, but the silence was worse than any poison she could have penned. At least as long as she had been writing, he knew she was alright. He had written so many apologies, begging her just to let him know she was alive, just one letter so he could breathe. But it never came. So he settled for his dreams, where she lay in his arms in a cottage so dark the stars shone like beacons.

For the last two hundred years his family had been enslaved by the Kyrons, generation after generation for a debt no one could even recall. His father had sworn never to have a child, to ensure the curse could not be passed on. The same vow that had been spoken by all his previous ancestors. Yet somehow an heir to the curse was always born. This was a feat in itself, given that preternaturals had difficulty continuing their lines.

Lord Kyron had gifted his mother to his father, ordering them to copulate each night until an heir was conceived. A second child may even have been ordered, if not for his mother dying a year after his birth. His father said she took her own life, that she had chosen to embrace death rather than watch her son be enslaved. It was only later he discovered that it had been her intention for both of them to die that day. But by some strange intervention, his life had been spared.

His father always claimed Lady Kyron had beseeched the spirits, asking that they save him so he could look after the child she knew she would one day conceive. Jesse.

He had known he was going to marry that girl since the day she first took his hand in hers and led him barefoot around the garden. It was a far more innocent time, a time when he hadn't understood that his blood made him nothing more than a plaything for her father, a throwaway shield. Even learning this hadn't changed the way he felt about her.

He remembered the day he was leaving, how she had beckoned him to bend so she might whisper in his ear. Instead, she had pressed her lips to his. There had been nothing but innocence behind the gesture, butterfly soft, a parting kiss between close friends destined to one day become more, but it became the kiss he had judged all others by, and he had found each one lacking.

As the outside scenery slowed, he saw the nostalgic view of the wind turbines in the distance, their forms reaching out towards the heavens, spinning freely while their solar-panel-lined blades created secondary generators of energy. Their hurried movement told tales of the racing wind that caressed the open plains, and all too soon the small station of Windmere came into view. His stomach sank.

For the last two years, he had been working covertly for Lord Kyron while still being pushed to his limits in training. Now he was here, it was as if his real sentence had begun.

There was but one glimmer of light in the bleak prospects that was his future, and that was the thought of seeing Jesse. Being tied to the Kyrons meant he was tied to her as well by something more than just his heart and soul. He wondered how the years had changed the eleven-year-old he had left behind.

CHAPTER 2

Jesse awoke in the embrace of pain to an unfamiliar sight. Her gaze desperately sought Levi, a small sigh escaping through her parched lips as he raised his head from beside her. She placed her hand to his fur, seeking comfort in a softness only she could feel as she examined her surroundings. The canopy of the wooden four-poster bed was draped with heavy, embroidered curtains. Pulled closed, they obscured her view of anything beyond, dulling the light and making it impossible to discern if it was night or day.

As she pushed herself up, the soft caress of silk against her legs caused an indignant heat to warm her cheeks. Someone had stripped her to the slinky, full-slip petticoat her father's maid had forced her into at his bequest.

It was no secret she was opposed to this marriage, but her father wanted to ensure she looked the part and that the groom received what he had paid for.

At any other time, she might have relished such a fine garment and the feel of the silk as it brushed against her skin. The way the hidden support lifted her breasts would have made it appear more like a summer dress if not for the delicate lace workings and the way it hugged her figure

Wincing, she slid herself across the enormous bed towards the drawn drapes. The way Levi lowered his head back to the mattress suggested they were alone. His black ears twitched just a moment before he rolled over, brushing his head against her arm the way he did whenever she was upset. Raising a hand to her cheek, she realised it was damp and cursed. Tears helped no one, they only brought more pain. She choked back a tiny sob. For just a brief moment, she had truly believed it was over, that she would escape.

As she slid her legs around her, she saw the white bandages binding her feet. The enchantments upon them normally brought a numbness to the pain, but all she could feel was fire. Levi nudged her again, his black ears twitching in a way that warned her time was running out. He looked up to her, his brown eyes filled with concern.

'I'm okay,' she assured him. It was true, she had suffered far worse than this, as the scarring on her arms, back, and legs would attribute. This pain was nothing, she reminded herself, parting the curtain to look through.

Her pulse quickened at the sight of bloody dressings and the tattered remains of her dress that lay discarded upon the polished wooden floor of what had to be the master bedroom. A room she had every intention of escaping.

A man's top hat and tails lay neatly folded on the ottoman beneath the large window. Her gaze lingered on it for a moment, watching how the light streamed through as if creating a beacon for her escape. Biting her lower lip, she drew in a long, steady breath through her nose.

She needed to move quietly, slowly, or risk alerting her newest captors. Giving into her fear, her panic, would only benefit them. Sliding her legs through the curtain, she hissed as fresh burning agony assailed her feet. Whatever poultice they had applied before the bandages squished between her toes as she gingerly applied more weight to her feet, using the large bed frame to guide her towards the wall.

The wooden wall panels had a rustic feel, their large overshadowing presence serving only to add further grandeur to the impressively sized room. It was far better in every way than her small prison with its bricked-up window, a place that had been barely large enough for her worn single bed. She limped feebly towards the glass panes, peering outside.

It was almost nightfall, and the sky had taken on that wondrous blue shade only visible as light faded to embrace the night. She looked up towards the clear sky, a fresh tear escaping her lashes.

'You never came. I begged you so many times and you never came.' She thought back to all the letters she had written to him after he left, how her maid would conceal them within the folds of her apron, and how each reply had caused her heart to quicken, until anticipation became disappointment and rejection.

She had hidden his replies within the small vent in the room that had become her prison. His scent had long faded, but she still remembered him. Even though he had stopped writing and moved on with his life, she never had.

Perhaps he had grown bored with her pleas, or just found himself something better. They had loved one another, but they had only been children.

She wiped her tears away. She had been a fool to think he would come. He had broken every promise he had ever made. Now was not the time to lose herself in wistful longings of what could have been.

She had written him one last letter, a final plea. If he had ever cared, she had implored him to find a way to stop the wedding. He hadn't come. She was alone. It was up to her now. She should have known better after ten years of silence. He had moved on, forgotten her. Today had cemented that in her mind once and for all. She had never meant as much to him as he had to her.

Pulling her gaze away from the sky, she searched for a means of escape. The property must have had a wraparound porch, sheltered from the elements if the small flat roof below was anything to go by. It wasn't too far a drop and, even without the roof, she would have jumped anyway. She had nothing left to lose. She fumbled with the window. Locked. Of course it was. She saw Levi tense, his hackles rising. She knew who was coming even before she heard his voice.

"I will be taking my daughter home now, Micah," barked her father from somewhere outside the large double doors. A cold sweat prickled her skin. She didn't know which was worse, being sold to a complete stranger or returning home with her father.

She glanced around, her gaze falling to the antique vanity table captured in the fading light from the window. It was bare, holding nothing she could use as a weapon. Hobbling over, she began to open drawer after drawer in silent desperation, wilfully silencing the whisper of the heavy wood sliding on the runners. Everything about this room sung of quality, but it was devoid of any personal touches, or anything she could use to defend herself.

"I think you'll find the contract you signed transferred possession of her to this clan. The moment you accepted payment this morning, she became mine to use as I see fit. With or without nuptials, she belongs to me." A deep voice rumbled. She struggled to swallow, her search becoming more desperate. She flung a nightgown over her shoulder to join the other discarded clothes in a pile on the floor. Another drawer now empty and another pit of despair grew in her turning stomach.

Please, give me something, a letter opener, a pencil, something, anything,' she implored silently, tossing aside the soft clothes from the next drawer until it too lay empty, and the patterned drawer lining seemed to mock her efforts with its bright and cheery colours. She grasped it in her hand, screwing it into a ball before hurling it across the room with all her might.

"Preposterous. Our deal is void. I failed to disclose her madness. I would be doing both of us a service to return her home." She glanced towards the door, her brow furrowed in confusion. Why would her father even care what became of her? Her trembling hands opened another drawer, smaller, empty.

Time was running out. She needed something now. Whatever the result of this argument, neither man had anything good planned for her. She would not subject herself to that life again. Not now, not when she could see freedom beckoning as the small twinkling of stars urged her on.

"Sanity has little to do with the plans I have for her. She doesn't need to be of sound mind to open her legs, and she is every inch the beauty you promised. I see no reason to renege. Even in light of this development I remain content with my purchase, as I am sure the rest of the men will agree." Tears prickled her eyes and her breath quickened. So that was it. He had sold her as a whore, again. She had to do something. This was her last chance. The moment that door opened, it was over. She started as she heard the handle rattle. Another drawer empty.

"Unacceptable—" The sound of a slight scuffle masked the sound of the next small drawer pulling free from its runners by her frustrated hand. She felt its weight. If this was all she had to work with, she would use it. Her breath quickened, her chest burning with fear as she hobbled towards the window.

"Lord Kyron, surely you do not intend to bring shame to our newly forged allegiance. I will interpret this outburst as a father mourning the loss of his only daughter. See the good lord out, my patience extends only so far."

She had reached the window by the time she heard the telltale click of the lock being released on the door. Raising the drawer above her head, she brought it down on the pane, time and time again, strike after ricocheting strike, her chest heaving. Levi warned of the figure's entrance just seconds before the thick doors slammed closed and the key rattled within the lock. She heard Levi's growling and hissing and could imagine him helplessly attempting to stall his advance. To anyone else he was just a spirit, unable to create an impact on the world of flesh no matter how hard he tried, and he always tried.

Firm hands seized her wrist, knocking the small wooden drawer from her grasp as she was forced to turn to face her new owner. Micah was a large man with dark hair and angry green eyes.

She screamed, pulling away, thrusting her weight to one side and the other, aware of the deafening cries of hysteria leaving her lips, aware of the pain in her ears from his own elevated voice as his gaze looked down upon her in fury. She knew how this would end; she had experienced it before. His vice-like grasp secured her wrists, dragging her towards the bed.

He was as strong as he was broad. The pain of her feet was all but forgotten as they scraped and kicked across the floor, trying to gain purchase until she felt herself flung on the mattress. At least it didn't screech, a part of her mind acknowledged. His lips were moving, but his words never reached her.

She didn't need to know what he was going to do to her. Nothing he said would be new. She had endured it all. Her arms lashed out, connecting weak strikes as panic rose within her. He was enormous, stronger in every way, but that didn't mean she was going to make this easy. She never did. He pressed his hand against her lips, muffling the sound of her screaming protests.

His weight straddled her as he pinned her on the bed. She bit and clawed as tears of fear betrayed her weakness. He towered over her like a bear, his oppressive form unresponsive to her struggles. She blinked, her heart pounding in her ears. It was then she saw it, the actual bear beside him.

Like Levi, its form was transparent, unseen by normal eyes. Without thinking, she grasped for it mentally, pulling it within herself, directing it back towards its owner. She heard Micah howl as she forced him into a partial shift before calling on his bear's strength.

She kicked out, this time throwing him off balance before

following through with a powerful blow to his temple, sending him tumbling backwards into the vanity table. Despite its sturdy frame, it collapsed under his hulking form. There was no time for her to question how she had done that, how she had overpowered a man easily twice her size and strength. She needed to get away before he rose.

Levi moved to stand beside her as she gasped breathlessly, tense, waiting to see if he would rise. When he didn't stir, and his form remained in partial shift, she advanced. Her trembling hands checked his pockets. A wallet. Good. She would need money. She continued to pat him down, fearful that any moment his shifted claws would slash out to detain her once more. What she really needed was —Levi trilled, his form reaching up the door towards the keys, still hanging from the inside of the lock from when he must have sealed them in.

The metal ring jingled in her grasp as she tried each tiny key in the window until finally one slid in place. She could hear him stirring behind her. It was now or never. Pushing open the sash window, she swung her legs outside, twisting on to her stomach as she lowered herself down.

Her gaze fixed before her on the forest. She would make it this time. She would find somewhere to hide, to rest, until she knew what to do. It would be dark soon, finding her would surely be impossible.

Micah groaned as he regained his internal balance, a wave of nausea encompassing him as his shifter's essence separated itself from him, allowing him to fully return to his humanoid form.

He had never heard of someone being able to do that, but the way her terrified gaze had fixed over his shoulder as she fought against him made him certain that what she had done had been no accident. Although the brief surprise across her features before she struck suggested it had been something even she herself was unaware she could do.

While slowly pushing into a seated position, he felt for the essence of his other-self, relieved to feel that, like himself, it was mostly unharmed. Few outside the shifter circle understood the dynamics of how their kind shifted. When they were born, they were two parts of the same being, animal and man, two beings of one heart and mind. At any point, only one could be in possession of the physical form.

When they chose to shift, the animal essence would replace the human one and by doing so the mortal form would shift, altering to take the shape of its new vessel. Their body was akin to a liquid during the transition, shaped by the dominant soul while their other-self stood near, like a ghost, unseen by everyone except others sharing the same ghostly realm.

He thought he had done his homework on this young woman, but information on her later life had been scarce. It had seemed straightforward. She had been born to her mother early, before her essence was ready, and the part of her that should have forged a solid bond with her other-self had not developed.

There was talk of this being a curse. She was the second child born on Lord Kyron's land who, at the age of seven—when their spirit form should have made itself known for their first joining—could not shift. What he hadn't anticipated, though, was her ability to be able to manipulate the essence of his own shifter. With a surge of adrenaline, he remembered her wild eyes as she fought against him, how they seemed to lock on his other-self and turn it against him.

When he had been researching her he had heard rumours of insanity, of how her father kept her locked away and had used any method he deemed fit to try to expel the demons from her. The scars he had seen were a testament to the abuse she had suffered at his hand, but he had never considered how deep that abuse had run.

The fear in her eyes as he tried to restrain her had caught him off guard. It had made him almost wish he hadn't grabbed her back from the tree. He had seen her flesh began to alter, becoming invisible against the bark as if nature itself was aiding her retreat. There was little doubt left in his mind she could see the world's spirits, just like her mother, Adeline Birch, could.

He winced, feeling the blood stream from his temple as the room finally stopped spinning enough for him to kneel. It was nothing a short spell in his other form wouldn't resolve. The cold draught from the window that caused the curtains to billow brought a new alarm to his diminishing confusion. He must have blacked out because she was no longer in the room.

"You alright, chief?" The doors sprang open and the loud bang as they struck the wall reverberated through his throbbing head as Dylan, his second in command, barged in. No doubt having returned from escorting Lord Kyron from the property just in time to hear the struggle within. Muttering a curse, Micah pushed himself to his feet, dashing towards the open window in time to see her straddling the perimeter wall. The fear in her posture as she glanced back to see him watching was unprecedented.

"Take Freya and bring her back. Just... be careful. Take the restraints." His second in command nodded, leaving him to sink on to his bed, his handkerchief pressed to his bleeding brow.

The coarse blanket of the forest's undergrowth tore at her bandages, but Jesse knew she would rather have the small barrier between it and her sore feet. She had endured worse than this, far worse, she reminded herself. A pitiful mantra, but it kept her situation in perspective, it kept her moving.

She was a fighter, that had always been her problem. Her father had said so countless times as he snapped his belt, or brought down his newest flogger. If only she would submit and be done with her madness, then she could become a daughter he was proud of, the heir he had wanted. She could never make him understand it wasn't insanity. He just didn't see the world the same way she did. No one did.

She had spent years locked within her bedroom, her chamber pot emptied twice daily. In that time, her father visited only when he needed to vent his ire or see if she had come to her senses.

Once she had pretended to change, but he saw the way her gaze would drift off into the distance. That day was the first time he had almost killed her. Deciding that expelling her demons through flagellation was no longer enough, he had sold her virginity to the highest bidder, hoping to completely break her and to bring her to leash with the threat of more violence.

He had tried to subdue her for fourteen years with fist, flogger, and rape, but some people were too stubborn to learn their lesson and know their place. The more he hurt her, the more she rebelled. Seeing his frustration and anger as she continued to defy him was one of her only triumphs. When all his methods failed, he decided he would sell her to a clan. By joining the two powers through marriage he hoped to establish his own heir, minus her madness. She knew there was more to his scheme, a reason why this wedding had needed to occur, but she was oblivious to the purpose. She only knew nothing good would come of it, for her at least.

She had known something was wrong when he hadn't taken the flogger to her for a moon's cycle and his second-in-command, Burnell, no longer visited when the lights were extinguished. Her father never once questioned the extra bruises, but part of her suspected he knew, even condoned it.

'*This way,*' Levi's reverberating meow encouraged, his large form weaving between smaller trees, guiding her towards a towering oak. Rain pattered upon the leaves, seeming almost like the rhythm of a drum keeping beat to nature's chorus as they sang in unison a celebration of life.

She stopped for a second, her hand upon the mighty trunk, its damp texture slick yet firm beneath her exhausted grasp. She was not made for this kind of endurance. Already, she could hear the sound of sodden boots, the trees combined with the rhythm of the rain making discerning their direction impossible, but they had gained so much ground on her already. She had come too far to give up now. She straightened, preparing to run when a hand emerged from the tree.

'To me, little druid,' the soft chime of a musical voice beckoned. She felt the pressure of her hand in another's even before she saw the beautiful visage of the tree spirit.

Moss, vine, and bark surrounded her womanly form, offering modesty while being completely alluring for the rare occasions they decided to show their face to mortals. But Jesse had always seen them, whether they wished to be observed or not.

Her leaf-coloured hair billowed in the wind as she pulled Jesse along towards another tree. 'Sit,' she commanded, and her tired legs had obeyed without question. For but a second the dryad disappeared into the bark of her tree, the portal between their two worlds, before her arms reached out, pulling Jesse against the solid trunk as her arms wrapped her in a tight embrace. 'Worry not, they will not find you here so long as you stay in contact with me and my home. Rest now, I will keep you safe this night.'

Jesse watched in tired amazement as her skin once more become transparent, but it was only as she moved she realised the truth. She was not invisible, but camouflaged. Her skin had become the same tones as her surroundings. She felt the dryad's fingers teasing through her hair briefly as she wove beautifully scented flowers within Jesse's damp and tangled locks.

Her head drooped, springing up as the sound of footfalls grew closer. She pressed her hands over her mouth, hoping to mask her panicked breathing. The heavy rain had caused the surroundings to mist, shrinking the visible world. At first, as the silhouettes of a cheetah and bear came into focus, she could not discern if they were mortal or incorporeal, not until she witnessed the slight golden hue surrounding them, a sign their mortal body was utilising some of their strength. A woman came into sight, her black hair clinging to her glistening dark skin. She walked with confidence; her steps light and movements as graceful as the large cat tethered to her. She turned full circle, searching the surroundings intently.

"She came this way, that's for certain." The softness of her voice surprised her. There was a warmth within the tones that no hunter should possess. The woman crouched, her hand to the ground while her vision probed her surroundings. Her gaze passed over where Jesse sat without hesitation. "I see no signs of tracks beyond this grove." She lifted her gaze to the treetops, searching their boughs and branches. Jesse watched her in awe. The woman looked like a primal goddess, hunting her quarry. She only wished she had not been the prey.

"Her scent is cold too," growled the other voice as another figure, broad and strong, emerged through the mists. "The chief isn't going to like this. Let's split up, circle around, see if we can find any trace."

"Then let's be quick, this rain's not our ally." Jesse listened to their slow departure, sitting in silence within the grove in the dryad's embrace. Above her, through the canopy of the trees, the clouds parted just long enough for her to see the stars. She wondered if Alec still looked at them too. Closing her eyes, she relished the feeling of the cold arms around her and allowed her mind to drift to her safe place, the one place that kept her sane through each and every trial.

The sweet smell of the blooming flowers in her mind were as real as if she were standing within a physical place. The spray of reds, purples, and blues brought her joy as she walked down the earth path towards the front door of the cottage.

Once inside, she was safe. No matter what occurred outside the doors of her mind she was no longer there. She was safe in these walls, in Alec's arms. As she closed the door behind her, she felt the warmth of his presence envelope her as his scent of cinnamon and ginger warmed her from within. There was nothing now, no danger, no pain, just his warm embrace. Here he held her close, protected her as he once promised he would.

He might have abandoned her in the real world but, in this corner of her mind, he was her strength, providing a sanctuary for her soul while the cruel and cold world outside tried to break her. He was the reason she never bent or broke to her father's will. His arms protected her while the stars outside shone brightly. This was her soul's sanctuary. The only place she felt safe.

'You must go now, little druid.' The gentle voice roused her, bringing her awareness back to the forest surrounding her. The sky was still heavy with rain and her damp body trembled against the chill. She wasn't sure how long she had slept, or when sleep had transitioned her from Alec's arms into dreams.

"How do I repay you?"

'Your presence was enough. Go now, my sisters say more are coming.' The dryad released her, gesturing forwards before sinking back through the tree into her realm.

Struggling to her feet, Jesse was aware of every ache and pain as she dusted the sodden debris from her clinging petticoat. The once soft texture now felt like ice on her flesh, deepening the chill expanding from her core. Her feet protested every step, but less than they had just yesterday. If nothing else, she healed quickly. She had to. If not, she was certain some of her father's beatings would have killed her. Being so close to Levi and the spirits always seemed to speed her own recuperation.

Her grasp tightened on the wallet, somehow still clutched within her grasp. Nothing was going to stop her this time. Nothing. She would keep moving until she found safety, people, a way out. The rain would mask her tracks and she was certain the flowers now tangled within her matted, mud-streaked hair had been placed there to disguise her scent. Even so, she knew better than to dally.

Her walk became a jog, her jog an agonising sprint until the forest's end became a great expanse of fields littered with vibrant wind turbines that caught the sun that now fought to drive back the rain as their solar-panelled blades spun silently.

In the distance she could see the small collection of buildings that created the shopping district of Windmere. She had not laid eyes upon it for years, but it still looked the same. Her vision drifted towards the railway station, the first definable building on the very border of the shopping district, as Levi encouraged her onward.

She needed only to board a train and she was free. No one would find her again, she could hide, become anyone she wanted. But first she had to get there. She pushed the pain to the back of her mind, the imaginary scent of ginger and cinnamon spurring her onward.

CHAPTER 3

*L*ord Kyron was fuming. His skin flushed almost as vibrantly as his red hair. This was not how things were meant to unfold. He had finally found a way to make his good-for-nothing daughter useful, only to discover that she was not as worthless as he had thought. The Alvar clan would pay for this.

They should have returned Jesse to him when the wedding was postponed. Instead, they escorted him from the property, refusing to return her to his arm. It was one insult too many. He was the lord of this town and his word was law. Yes, he *had* sold her to the clan, but that was before he'd known the truth, before he'd realised what she could do. All these years he had thought she was mad, insane, just like her mother. If only he'd known the truth.

If his had been the hands that had seized her, he would have dragged her back home. He would have left with her before they'd had a chance to stop him. But no, it had been him. That accursed Alvar clan's alpha. The second that woman, Freya, had descended the staircase and spoken in Micah's ear, he had seen his chance. The whisper of scarring had morphed his expression from defiance to rage as he no doubt realised the promised beauty had been damaged and sullied.

If fate had been with him, Micah would have renounced his claim upon her there and then. Instead, he had thundered upstairs and ensured that he could not gain access to his own child. He couldn't even tempt him with dissolution of contract.

Damn that contract. If not for that, he would have had the Blue Coats bring her home. He should have stipulated that an exchange of vows had to occur, but at the time he was too concerned with getting the reluctant bride to cooperate. What kind of daughter ensured their father had to drug them so a maid could dress her in semi-compliance for her wedding?

That damn child had been a thorn in his side for years. Her will was forged of steel. No matter what he subjected her to, she defied him, resisted him. All he had wanted was for her to stop seeing through the eyes of madness. Why couldn't she have just fallen into line? It was for this reason he ensured the power he had negotiated for would remain his, wedding be damned. It had come at too opportune a time to refuse the offer, at the time he most needed funds to extend his influence further.

What a fool he had been. But still, it wasn't his fault. Jesse had never displayed any signs of being able to do anything spectacular. She had simply held one-sided conversations with herself and spent more time in her world of fantasy than in the real one.

Perhaps the fact he had never broken her spirit should have alerted him to her unusual nature. He had forced stronger creatures to his will by his belt alone. He had intended to make her meek, controllable, yet she fought him at every turn, no matter what he did. He saw part of her defiance waver when she thought his servant had stopped writing.

That had been a brilliant scheme by Martha. She'd said the two shared a deep connection, that he should allow them to exchange letters under his nose, allowing her to gain faith and comfort as their bond continued to grow, only for him to sever it at the most opportune time. He liked the idea of giving her hope only to strip it away later, causing them both distress. Pain made people easier to control, after all, and Alec had also needed to be brought to heel.

He had relished in her anguish. She had been more subdued as her letters continued to go unanswered, not quite broken, but it would have been enough for what he now had in mind. Back then, he had merely wanted to break her will, to make her into the submissive, meek, obedient woman her mother should have been.

He knew he was making progress when finally, two years ago, her letters to him stopped. But within days of throwing out her papers, her defiance sparked again and her fight began anew. Had he known then what she would be capable of, he would have bound her. But the chance had not slipped him by yet. He had seen her fleeing as he drove away from the Alvar mansion. All was not lost. Not so long as he found her first. There was only one place his daughter would run, and when he was done with her this time, it wouldn't matter who possessed her body, she would be his in soul.

Jesse's feet were burning, her bandages shredded beyond any measure of protection as she reached the railway station. The platform was exactly what would be expected in a minor town; small, well-maintained and almost deserted. The ticket office stood near the entrance to the stone platform where there was a cosy sit-in cafe, and benches grouped beneath the small shelter that were currently virtually empty. It was almost the same as she remembered when last she saw it over fourteen years ago.

Sometimes, after school, Alec would bring her to this café and they would sit at their table, the first table by the door, the only place where the decorative windows didn't obscure the view of the outside world. A young couple was currently sitting there talking, their forms distorted by the steamed windows. They looked happy, just as she and Alec would have to anyone passing by.

He would always buy an ice cream or dessert for them to share, something as sweet and delicious as he had been. Whenever he looked away, she would smear just a trace near her lips, knowing he would reach across and wipe it away with his thumb. The way he touched her made her heart sing, and she loved nothing more than to watch his eyes sparkle as he brought his thumb to his mouth to taste the sweetness. Nothing had looked sexier. Except, perhaps, his boyish grin.

He had this way of making her feel safe, as if she was the only person in the world. A few days before his fourteenth birthday, as they sat drawing faces in the window's condensation, and watching the water chase the path traced by their fingers, he had taken her hand in his.

She still remembered how her breath had frozen while his eyes studied her bruised face with a serious expression that held an age beyond his years. He had spoken softly, yet his words had engraved themselves into her heart and soul. He told her that one day he would take her away from this town, away from her father, never to return.

He had promised.

He had looked her in the eyes and lied.

She had waited for that day, but it never came. His letters had given her hope that he still thought of her after her father had sent him away to study. Her stomach tightened as she remembered how he abandoned her, how she had written to him when her father's fists had no longer been enough, and he had slid his belt from his trousers, beating her until she had lost consciousness, until she awoke streaked in blood.

That was when his replies stopped. She begged him to come and take her away. She poured her heart into the ink, yet each month no reply would come. For the last two years she hadn't been able to pick up a pen, not until she discovered she was being forced to wed. Only then had she written one final plea. Begging him to come for her one last time. He never did.

Jesse froze, aware of the unusual stares she was attracting. It was doubtful, even with fashion trends and summer's approach, that seeing a young woman running around in a rain-drenched slip with bare feet and bloody bandages would be an everyday occurrence. She was exhausted. She didn't care, they could stare all they wanted, this was far from her worst humiliation. She was leaving. She just needed a ticket and then she could sink into obscurity. She leaned against the ticket booth, her sweat disguised by the dampness of rain upon her flushed skin.

To her right, Levi growled, nudging her hand with his head, making sure she was aware of the threat. She stroked her fingers over his head, knowing how odd a woman stroking air would seem to anyone watching.

Despite her fatigue, she had seen them. The three men dressed in dark clothes whose muscles had tensed ever so slightly as their gaze passed over her casually. They sat apart, their body language suggesting they were strangers, but the way their shifter essences played together in the spirit realm betrayed their pretence. They had no way of knowing their essences would behave in such a manner, not unless they'd realised this realm could host private conversations between alike essences. From what she had witnessed, most shifters were unaware of this, choosing to keep their own awareness in the eyes of their shifter side instead of exploring the realm in which they awaited transition.

Heat flushed her face as the brown-haired woman in the ticket booth cleared her throat only to acknowledge her with a disapproving glance over her stylish glasses. Jesse peered inside the stolen wallet before looking to the digital screen on the wall behind the bored, judgemental woman inside, her open mouth gum chewing creating a smacking sound that echoed around the brick small hut as she waited for her to speak.

She knew she needed to get as far away from here as possible, but she couldn't risk using all her funds, it was doubtful anyone would even entertain hiring her looking like this. Her vision panned down the destinations and prices before glancing back towards where the men were seated.

Her heart missed a beat. There were only two now. They were standing, watching her, approaching. She could hear the clatter of the train in the distance, the whistle alerting passengers of its arrival. Surely they were just getting on. Her breathing quickened as the first man's foot passed the boarding area. The way in which his eyes were fixed on her caused her throat to swell.

"Well, do ya want a ticket or not? Train's pulling in." She sounded as if speaking to her had left a nasty taste in her mouth. She peered down her nose at her again before sucking on the gum to make it pop. "Well?"

"Erm." She saw the other man had also passed the boarding dock, but where was the third? They had to be Micah's men. Of course he would figure out she was going to go the railway station, it was the only way she could leave this town. The only transport running on a Sunday. "I-I've changed my mind. I—" She backed away, her eyes on the two approaching men, turning sharply she let out a yelp, almost colliding with the third man who had somehow flanked her.

The scream escaped her lips the same time as the train doors hissed open. If they were going to snatch her, it would be now. The crowd was thin, but enough to—the man tapped his belt, bringing her attention to the knife handle. Stepping back she saw the other two had blocked her path to the train. "Excuse me," she stepped around the single figure, hoping they wouldn't risk exposure in front of the young woman.

She had barely taken a step when the foot traffic began filtering from the train. Glancing over her shoulder, she confirmed it was as she feared, they were following. Her pulse quickened with her pace as she noticed Levi was no longer beside her.

Her pursuers were armed with knives and who knew what else. Were their instructions to return her alive, or did Micah only care about reclaiming what was his? She thought back to his crushing touch as he'd grabbed her and found her legs pumping harder. She was not going back. She would die first.

Sweat trickled down her brow, mingling with the cool mist of the rain. It had been years since she had last seen the city, or walked its streets. She recalled walking hand in hand from school with Alec, cutting through the—her vision scanned the street, finding the alley that led to the more populated area of town. There she could duck into a busy shop, buy clothes, find help, a Blue Coat maybe. But what if Micah had reported the assault? She would be apprehended and delivered back to him as soon as he presented the clan contract.

Like it or not, she was part of his clan now. If she were to be caught, she would wind up in his clutches. She had not gone through all this, finally had a taste of freedom, only to be returned into a life of service where—how had he put it—*'she doesn't need to be of sound mind to open her legs.'* No, thank you.

She didn't escape one tyrant only to find herself with another. She needed clothes, quickly, people were bound to take notice of a woman running the streets in her underwear. If only she could get to the main pavilion she could seek shelter until it was safe and emerge dressed. She could even spin a story about a peer prank. She'd read in some of her books people her age sometimes got drunk and played such tricks on friends. But first she needed to put some distance between herself and the three men.

As she took off through the alley, she could still feel their presence behind her. But she was moving fast, while they still walked grouped together, marching with hurried steps, but not enough to draw attention to the three men who were about to follow a half-naked young woman into an alley.

She heard their heavy boots on the cobblestones as they reached its entrance, and quickened her own pace. Their reluctance to simply seize her in public suggested they didn't want to be noticed. And if they thought she was going to go quietly, they had another think coming.

She winced as shards of shattered glass embedded themselves

into one of her bare feet, a slight hop to brush her sole down her leg and it was gone, leaving a cut across her leg and an open wound ready to be infected by whatever substance made this stone entryway feel somehow both slick and sticky. She crinkled her nose against the smell, pushing herself onward, ignoring the pain. She had endured worse.

Metal wire woven into a chain-link barricade crossed the brick alleyway. She ran into it, her fingers curling around the metal chains desperately. This couldn't be happening. When did they put this here? Her hands grasped the gate desperately, pulling it firmly, once, twice, three times. Nothing, no give, no way to squeeze through the smallest gap between the gate and fence.

No, this shouldn't be here, they'd always cut through here to sneak across behind the delivery port. The slight rusting of the lock as she tugged against it, hoping to force it loose suggested this was not a new development.

She cursed her foolishness. How could she have believed nothing had changed in fourteen years?

Without daring to look over her shoulder, she put her hands to the metal and began to climb, unsure if the pounding she could hear was her heart or the footsteps of her pursuers. She ignored the pain of the metal biting into her bleeding feet as she pushed her bare toes between them. Something wrapped around her throat. For a moment, as she screamed, she thought it was a rope like the one her father had used to stage her mother's suicide. But it was something worse, much worse. At least death was still an escape. She felt a sharp tug on the collar as she was pulled back and flung to the floor so hard the air whooshed from her lungs.

Shards of moss-coated glass burned her back as she slid across the rough ground but, instead of focusing on the pain, on how raspy her breathing sounded as she pulled it in through bared teeth, her hand reached out, seeking the jagged remains of the ancient bottle, smashing it against the face of figure who'd bent to grab her.

He staggered backwards as the broken bottle hit him, leaving blood flowing from his wound. He swore, backing away, cupping his face as someone else's foot connected with her ribs. Crying out, she prayed someone would hear. But she knew better by now. No one ever heard her screams, they might as well have been silent.

A sharp tug caused her eyes to mist. Pain burned across her scalp as someone grabbed a fistful of her hair, dragging her to her knees before him. She choked. Her own hands, instead of grasping his, moved to the collar, trying to pry it free. She felt its solid band, seamless, as her broken fingernails sank into her flesh as she tried to claw it free. How the hell had this thing been snapped so easily into place when it was so solid? The arms of the third man, the blond one, grasped her arms, forcing them behind her back.

"What do you say, boys?" said the dark-haired thug gripping her hair. He pushed his crotch toward her face, laughing as she tried to turn away. "Shall we make her apologise to us real nicely like?"

She gasped as he pulled her hair again, wrenching her head backwards. Unfortunately for him, she'd been in this position before, but she was a fighter, not a victim. She cried out, thrusting her head forwards, head-butting him. The dark-haired man before her howled, his hand coming away with clumps of hair.

Rolling to the side, she used the surprise to wrench her arms free, bringing her legs around in a sweeping motion as she tried to get to her knees. The blond man's fingers secured her ankle, pulling her towards him. Without thinking, she kicked his hand, still ignoring the pain as she tried to slacken his grasp.

Another foot connected with her ribs. She'd lost track of where everyone was. Everything was a blur of limbs grasping and clawing at her until an oppressive weight straddled her. The cool bite of metal at her throat stilled her struggle. The face above her was twisted into a sneer that somehow made the trickle of blood and shattered glass dust on his face look menacing. She was going to pay for that, was what his gaze warned.

"That's quite enough of that," he snarled. He pinned her arms beneath his legs, snatching the knife to cut one of the straps of her petticoat before pressing the knife's tip just hard enough to draw blood as he traced its blade down towards her heaving breasts. Levi's sudden deep rumbling growl brought little comfort. She'd rather he ran, that he didn't try to engage with three attackers' essences for her. His ears were pressed flat against his head, his gaze fixed towards the entry to the alley.

Remembering what happened with Micah, spurred on by Levi's appearance, Jesse reached out mentally, desperately searching for her attackers' shifter essences, praying she could draw upon them again. It was her only hope, her only chance. But the aura of her attackers remained invisible.

It was then, with alarm, she realised the only creature she could feel was Levi.

Whatever the collar was they had affixed to her, somehow blocked her interaction with everything but him.

The slowing of the train had been just the excuse Alec had needed to move. Grabbing his backpack from the overhead shelf, he left the lawyer partway through whatever he had been wittering on about. He didn't need to hear what he had to say. He had heard it more times than he could count. It wasn't as if anything changed because he was physically in Lord Kyron's presence.

His chest tightened with the squealing of the brakes. He had fought to return so many times and foolishly had always thought she would be waiting for him.

In his mind she would be standing on the platform, a vision of beauty, their eyes would meet and the crowd divided so he could run to her, taking her in his arms, hearing her laugh as he spun her around in his firm embrace before he stole her away from this town forever and made her his.

But she had moved on.

She was getting married.

He glanced towards his watch with a sigh. No, she was already married. His shoulder jolted another passenger as he made his way towards the door and, despite it being his fault, the person shied from his angry stare, apologising.

He pushed a hand through his hair, inadvertently adding a little more volume to its choppy, stylish cut, before grasping the rail as the train slowed. His gaze fixed to the approaching platform, his heart quickening as if it still dared to hope.

As the brakes of the train screamed harder, he snorted in disdain, seeing a group of well-dressed men at the station rise. For a fleeting second he thought they were there to collect him, but then he recalled something else the lawyer had said. The entire household was being granted a week's leave in celebration of his daughter's wedding. While he was expected to be in town, he had some free time before he was to report for duty.

These had been the first words from the lawyer's lips as they had boarded the train in the early hours of this morning. It had taken every ounce of his restraint not to wipe that condescending sneer from the lawyer's thin lips as he delivered the gut-wrenching blow. He got it, they'd made sure he'd seen the announcement of the wedding. She'd moved on. She'd moved on without him. He felt his hand rubbing his chest as the familiar ache returned.

It was only a few seconds after they stood he realised the suits really weren't there for him. Their focus was being completely held by someone else, a young woman.

His heart skipped. It couldn't be.

He blinked once, twice, three times.

It was.

Dressed in some sensual summer dress, soaked to the bone, with her honey-coloured hair plastered across her bare skin, was Jesse. His hand massaged his chest again, this time as a reminder to breathe. Could she really be here to meet him? His heart skipped a beat at the thought.

The doors were barely open when he squeezed between them,

scanning the platform, looking to catch sight of her. But she was gone. A ghost, nothing more than a figment of his imagination.

Exhaling a shaky breath he emerged from the station, masking his disappointment as he slung his backpack over his shoulder while scanning the streets that had once been his home. The glimpse of the three quick-marching suits crossing the road rekindled his hope. If they were real, then maybe she had been too. A brief flash of honey coloured hair barely caught his sight just moments before the figure vanished into the alleyway. Their alleyway.

His heart beat harder and louder than ever before. It was her, it had to be. He could feel it. His boots echoed on the asphalt as he pursued. He was only moments behind her, closer than he had been for years. Anger tensed his every muscle as he saw her, pinned to the ground while one of the suits, now sporting a bloody face, traced a knife across her chest, leaving a slight red trail.

He growled. His feet carried him without thought as his years of training took over. His elbow connected to the chin of a dark-haired man who'd been nursing his groin, and his head snapped back into the alleyway's wall before he had time to even register the approaching danger.

Alec was quick, smooth, and graceful from years of training. Ducking, he evaded a blow from the blond-haired assailant, connecting a staggering stomach punch before striking his temples. In seconds, the two men had fallen. He slipped the knife from the blond man's belt, about to bring it to the third assailant's throat when the brute on top of her suddenly lost his balance as she twisted beneath him.

He saw the knife cut deeper into her flesh, but she fought through the pain, bringing her outside leg over his ankle pushing him as she twisted, curling her body to slide out beneath his arm. Seeing the opening, he slid the knife across the man's throat in a smooth motion, one which sang of the countless times he had practised this execution.

Jesse pulled herself into a predatory crouch, blood spattered across her already filthy skin making her look feral and dangerous as her blue eyes looked towards him, sizing him up, measuring his threat with a gaze so cold it changed her very features. She faltered slightly, her other arm rising to cradle her midriff as her gaze lifted from the weapon in his hand to his face. It only took a moment for her cold, steely gaze to soften, and any anger he had harboured towards her to melt.

"Alec?" The pain in her voice betrayed the mask she wore. He crouched, his knuckles gently tracing the contour of her jaw as he held her gaze. "You came?" That was what it sounded like she had said as she slid her hand into his, accepting his help.

He released a breath as their skin touched, a breath he had been holding for fourteen years. She hissed, not quite straightening. Her gaze searched his face, her hand raising as if to touch him, but her fingers closed, her hand lowered. "I can't believe you really came." Her knees buckled beneath her, her eyes fluttering closed as her body grew limp.

Scooping her into his arms, he held her close. She was filthy from head to toe, soaking wet and covered in a layer of dirt and blood. She had left him without a word for ten years, he reminded himself as his eyes began to burn. She gave up, moved on, she was married, he listed each point mentally, all too aware of the loudest voice of all was the one that whispered with quiet relief, she was in his arms, he was finally home.

CHAPTER 4

Alec had changed so much from the teenager who had been sent away, but she had recognised him in less than a heartbeat. He was the only person who was connected to her, a tether invisible to all, a single silver strand linking her heart to his. At some point, in his arms, she had fallen asleep, or lost consciousness. She wasn't sure which. The events were a blur of confusion. She remembered meeting his eyes and the overwhelming feeling of relief, the way her soul had sagged as their hands touched, then nothing until she awoke here.

For a moment, she had feared it had all been a dream, a retreat into the safe place of her mind where he always waited to hold her. But as she opened her eyes, there he was, standing silhouetted against the rain-streaked window. The years had been so kind, sculpting the attractive teenager into the kind of man who made women swoon. His brown hair had been styled to draw focus to his long-lashed honey-coloured eyes, while its choppy-textured tempted her fingers into reaching out to bury themselves into it.

He watched her intently, his brow drawn down into an expression she couldn't quite read. Levi stood beside the bed between them, growling, his eyes piercing Alec with such intensity she wondered if he could feel the glare penetrating the realms.

As soon as he had noticed her eyes were open, he pushed himself up from the windowsill, leaving silently, without even a word. Her heart sank. He had done exactly what she had asked him to do, and now he was leaving, again. She wanted to shout after him, to ask him to stay, to ask him why he had stopped writing, but her voice froze and the only sound to follow him was that of the door locking behind him.

She rubbed her tight chest with her fingers, trying to find the strength to let him go. Trying to convince herself that the fact he had come at all should have been enough. But it wasn't. She'd seen him now, and for the first time in fourteen years, for the briefest moment, she had felt... something, something peaceful, she'd felt at ease, safe, a feeling that had escaped her for the longest time.

She sucked a deep breath through her teeth as she pushed herself from the bed, hobbling across the redwood flooring towards the bathroom. Part of her had been tempted to roll over, to sink back into oblivion, but she didn't know how much time she'd have before someone found her, and the smell of the earth and decay on her flesh warned of pending infections and complications she couldn't afford on the run.

Part of her resisted, not wanting to lose the slightest hint of his scent still upon her skin from when he had held her, but she knew first-hand how important clean wounds were. She traced her fingers around the collar. She'd need something to keep this hidden sooner rather than later. Micah had ensured running wouldn't be easy. Anyone seeing this would know she belonged to a clan who would be actively seeking her return.

She sat in the bath, using the shower head to rinse the debris from her body, watching in tired detachment as small flowers and crystal droplets from her hair raced towards the plughole, spiralling with the brown stained water until finally it ran clear. Streams of blood left her feet as she pulled embedded pebbles, thorns, and glass from her skin until the clear water ran pink.

Only once she had removed every trace of filth and blood from her skin and hair with the toiletries provided, did her trembling hands plug the bath, turning on the thermostat and jets as it filled. Lifting her water-soaked hair over the edge, she leaned back, leaving the complimentary conditioner on her tangled locks as she relaxed. Lifting her legs to rest upon the edges of the claw-foot bath to avoid submerging her feet she allowed her hair to cascade loosely over the other side to making a soft pattering sound upon the wet-room floor that almost beat in time with the rain.

The gentle hum of the thermostat as it kept the water at her chosen temperature, combined with the vibrations from the jets, was like a lullaby. The churning water made the generous quantities of richly scented bubbles rise, threatening to escape over the edge with her every movement.

Her muscles felt weary as the warmth enveloping her mingled with the beautiful fragrances that calmed her mind and body. Relaxing, she exhaled, relishing the embrace of the heated cradle. Her heavy eyelids threatened to close as she watched the plumes of steam rise to mist the air in the tiled room. It was doubtful she could move now, even if she wanted to. Once burning with exhaustion, her limbs had now grown heavy. There was so much she needed to think about, so much she needed to do, but the only thought in her mind as she lay back was that Alec had come.

She wasn't sure how long she was asleep, but she heard the soft sigh escape her lips as she felt a gentle caress upon her scalp. The relaxing sensation took her back to her childhood, to the days she would lie in the bath and her mother would wash her hair, and how after her mother had died Alec had taken over this task.

She allowed herself to sink into the dream, into the tender touch as fingers stroked her hair. Warm water soothed her sore scalp, and the sound of it spilling to the tiled floor tore her from the dream. Her heart sped as she realised the touch remained, the sounds and sensations lingered beyond the longing of a dream. Suddenly awake, she sucked in a startled gasp, her arms flailing. Two hands grasped her in time to stop her from going under, and still she fought, water cascading with bubbles from the bath splashing loudly against the tiles.

"Jess." The sonorous voice soothed, his husky tone calming her panic slightly. His grip tightened around her. "Hold still." Panting for breath, she put her feet in the tub, biting down on her lip to prevent herself from crying out as the water stung her wounds anew. But her pulse raced from more than just the fright, he'd come back. "Hey, I've got you," he soothed. "I've got you." After a few moments, she felt his hold on her release as his fingers returned to her hair.

"Zounds, Alec, you scared me half to death." She tried her best to still her ragged breathing, but no sooner had her fear calmed her cheeks flushed for an entirely different reason. She turned her head, peering at him through the corner of her eyes. He sat on a small chair at the head of the bath, a wide-toothed comb in his grasp and an amused expression on his face. "Pass me the towel."

"Hold still, I've nearly finished." She placed her hands across her chest, her stomach fluttering as he gave a deep chuckle. "Relax, your modesty is preserved." She glanced down to the thick lather of bubbles still filling the tub and relaxed a little, allowing herself to enjoy his attention.

She couldn't remember the last time anyone had treated her with such care. She raised her hand, wiping her damp eyes, hoping he hadn't seen the tears such tenderness had spurred. "There, all done. There's a clean shirt on the bed, but I'll be treating your cuts and bruises first. Come, sit." She stared at him incredulously as he stood, gesturing towards the wooden cantilever chair that belonged to the small two-seater table in the main room. "Under your own steam or mine, Jess. Don't make me drag you from the bath."

"I can see to myself." Her reply was more clipped than she had intended. She raised her gaze to his. The bath suddenly became too warm as she saw him standing there, arms crossed, gazing at her with the most intense stare she had ever seen. Despite the slightest twitch of his lips as her skin flushed, she knew he wasn't taking no for an answer. "Fine, step outside so I can at least cover up."

"I'll turn my back," he conceded. And he did, giving her the perfect opportunity to study his ass. "Now, Jess." Wincing, she stepped from the bath, leaving pink stains on the grey tiles in her wake as she limped painfully across the wet room's floor to grasp the towel. It was barely big enough to wrap around herself.

She grabbed the second one, no larger than a dishcloth, patting herself dry, aware of every minor abrasion. Placing it on the seat, she sat awkwardly, her arms resting on the chair back as she straddled it. Her worst scrapes were on her back, from the glass on the ground in the alleyway. Well, her back and feet. At least the back of the chair shielding her front would preserve a little of her modesty. "You ready?" She made a small noise, it was all she could manage. Moving to the sink, he grabbed a bag with a pharmacy logo printed on it.

She swallowed as his fingertips brushed her hair aside with a featherlight touch before he tugged at the towel, freeing it from her back. It was only a second of hesitation, but she felt him freeze, the air pressure changed, and suddenly she found it difficult to breathe. She tensed, her breath hitching as she immediately regretting giving in to his wishes. She could only imagine what he felt looking upon her, revulsion, disgust, the same things she herself saw as she gazed upon her scared flesh in her old bedroom filled with mirrors. She grasped for the towel, attempting to cover herself up.

"Don't," he growled in a low whisper. She flinched as she felt his fingers on her flesh. What had she been thinking letting him see this? She shied from his touch, her breathing frozen as his fingers traced the criss-cross marking that marred her skin. "Don't." There was a heartache to his voice that caused her eyes to mist with tears. As she seized the towel, his hand grasped hers. She could see the fierce emotions as, with a set jaw, he studied the long-healed lacerations also covering her arms as her cheeks flushed with shame. Her vision dropped to the tiles, unable even to look at him.

These horrific markings had been the reason her wedding dress had been designed with both a high back and long sleeves. It was to hide the damage her father and Burnell had enjoyed inflicting on her over the years.

She shuddered as he touched her again, biting her lip to prevent her teeth from chattering as adrenaline caused her temperature to plummet. His touch was firmer this time, caressing her wounds as if he thought his touch alone could erase them. As she melted into his touch, she almost felt as if it could. Her head drooped forwards and the only sensation became the pleasure of his caress, mingled with tiny explosions of pain as his fingertips found raw abrasions, cuts, and the forming bruises.

His touch stirred a warmth in her stomach, the tenderness causing a lump to rise within her throat that made swallowing almost impossible. She felt her adrenaline dip, her body giving in to fatigue under the influence of the soothing caress. She was barely aware of anything through the haze of exhaustion until his rough fingers traced across her shoulder as he moved to stand before her, lifting her chin with his fingers. She looked at him through heavy eyelids, her breathing once more quickening as he placed a hand to her chest. Until that moment, she had all but forgotten the shallow knife wound. He dressed it carefully with the same delicate and attentive touch, his silent rage simmering. He still looked like her protector. The boy she had loved stood before her a man. The same man who had abandoned her.

Alec bit back the questions. There was no point asking what he already knew. He had studied each and every wound, every mark, every blemish. As a child, he had wanted nothing more than to protect her. After all, that was what a man should do, protect anyone who needed it. But it had always been different with Jesse, more primal, a need that ran deeper. He could see there had been more than her father's hand at work and dared not dwell on the thoughts of what she had endured.

He cursed himself silently. He should have tried harder to get back to her. No, he shouldn't have tried, he should have done it. He had failed her, broken each and every promise he had ever made. Adeline, Jesse's mother, had asked only one thing of him, that he make her happy. Soul-bonded, that was the word she had used for what he and Jesse were. She had been planning to free him the night she was murdered, the first night Jesse had witnessed her father's wrath.

The few bruises he had treated before leaving were nothing compared to those she bore now, and each one cut him to the core. Each one told him of his failure. But she was here now, safe and, husband be damned, he wouldn't let anyone take her from him again.

He opened the door to the bathroom, managing a weak smile as she wrapped the towel around herself, teetering into the bedroom as if he hadn't seen her undressed countless times. But it was different now. She was no longer a child, she was every bit the woman he knew she would grow to become. The vision of the woman he held in his dreams.

He closed the bathroom door, breathing in the cool mist left from her bath. He needed a moment. Walking towards the mirror he wiped his hand across its foggy surface, to see his own angry glare staring back. This was not a face she needed to see.

His mind lingered on the image of her in the alleyway, of how she had fought. There was nothing trained or disciplined behind her actions, not like when he moved. She had learnt to survive, to use her slight frame in ways people wouldn't expect. There was only one way to learn to fight like that. Experience. He grasped the toothbrush glass and flung it against the wall, creating a rain of shards. His hand gripped the sink as he glared at the highly polished plughole, taking breath after breath until he regained his composure.

When he emerged, she had already slipped into the shirt he had left for her on the bed. It was far too large, falling to rest just above her knees, and by the gods did she look sexy. How was it his clothes looked better on her? He could keep her like that forever, dressed in only his clothes, his own scent lingering on her flesh. He bit back a growl, scolding himself for the invading thoughts, while his own body betrayed him, making his longing for her clear. She had been nothing more than a fantasy for years, and now she stood before him, every inch his goddess, it was all he could do not to claim her for his own.

"Lie down," he commanded, seeing the exhaustion on her face. She seemed to hesitate for a moment before lying on the bed. It warmed his heart. After everything she had endured, she still knew beyond a shadow of a doubt she could trust him. He sat at the base of the bed, resting against the wooden footboard as he pulled more items from the bag and began gently to rub her feet. "You stopped writing," he whispered. He hadn't meant for her to hear. It had been a thought put to voice before he could help himself. She pushed herself up onto her elbows, her eyes piercing his with anger.

"What was the point of writing when you never replied?" The bite in her voice surprised him.

"Whoa, Jess." He lifted his gaze from her feet, his eyes fixed to hers. He knew how to read people, and she believed every word she had just spoken. "I wrote to you. I wrote to you so many times. For ten years, even though you never replied. For ten years after you told me he'd struck you with his belt, I begged you to tell me you were okay. I pleaded. But I never received a response. There were times I thought you were dead, Jess. Then, just before I was due to return, I found out you weren't just alive, you were getting married."

"I... oh, Alec." His heart ached as he watched her cover her face to hide her tears. "I only stopped writing two years ago. I thought you were here because, because I wrote one final time asking for your help," she sniffled.

"Clearly we've both been played for fools. I never gave up on you." He did well to hide his anger. Ten years of frustration. Ten years of her thinking she was alone, thinking he had abandoned her, that he had let her down. But each thought in that list was true.

She had been alone and abandoned, and he had let her down.

She didn't receive his letters, but that didn't change the fact he hadn't saved her. "Now, tell me, what is a newly married woman doing roaming the streets in such a state? Where is your husband?" he asked, although he didn't really care about whom she had married, only what had happened to her, and whose face his enraged fists needed to find for letting her come to such harm. What kind of man let a woman like her suffer this way? Whoever married her should be overjoyed, not turning a blind eye while she was attacked in the streets, looking as though she'd been through hell. She deserved to be loved, treasured.

He listened as she spoke, rubbing the soothing ointment into the soles of her feet with a feather-light touch. His fingers and thumbs worked delicately to ease just a fraction of her pain. She lay back, staring at the ceiling, her arm across her eyes as she relived the last twenty-four hours.

He pressed his lips together, focusing on keeping his touch soft, on pretending not to see the glistening of tears she thought her arm disguised. But no matter how hard he tried, he couldn't push away his feelings of failure as his gaze strayed to the scars. Each and every one she had suffered was because he had failed her.

He wrapped the special bandages with a practised hand and even managed to pretend that the way she rolled on her side, turning her back to him the moment his grasp released, did not affect him so deeply. Instead, he crawled on to the soft mattress behind her, covering them in the soft duvet while he folded his arm around her protectively, pulling her towards him as he had done many times before, both before they parted and in his dreams.

His fingers gently stroked her arm and, while he held her, breathing in the scent of home, and his own heart began to heal just a little in her presence as her quiet tears were replaced by the slow rhythm of breathing as she drifted into slumber.

He was angry but, more than that, he knew he could not fail her again. He needed to get her away from this town to somewhere safe, somewhere beyond her father's reach where no one would think to look for her. He couldn't believe she had escaped one tyrant only to be sold to another.

No more.

She would suffer no more. He tightened his grasp on her protectively, pulling her closer. He would do now what he had been too young to do back then. He would protect her.

Jesse awoke to the feeling of Alec's arm wrapped around her, his warm breath tickling her exposed neck as each breath caused his slight stubble to prickle against her shoulder. This feeling, this safety, it eclipsed anything she thought she'd found in the recess of her mind.

Moonlight streamed through the small gap in the curtains, bringing a cool glow to the otherwise darkened room. She stared at the door, wondering if she could slip from his embrace, free him from his obligation of staying. But then she remembered the last ten years had been a lie.

All the anger and betrayal, all the heartache she had felt from each unanswered letter, had been by her father's design, of this she was certain. Had he seen how she felt about him, had he orchestrated her abandonment thinking she would simply wither?

Her bladder ached, reminding her of the desperate need that had roused her from the most peaceful sleep she had known for a long time. As she slid from beneath his arm, she heard him groan in his sleep. Her bandaged feet throbbed as she placed them to the floor, disrupting the moment.

Later, she told them. She could feel their pain later.

For now, she wanted to bask in the lingering sensation of his warmth still upon her flesh. She brushed a tear from her eye, hating how emotional the last few days had made her, and clicked the bathroom door closed. She had dreamt of him so many times, of him coming to her rescue, she feared she would soon awake to find herself wed and imprisoned once more.

As she relieved herself, her vision strayed to the backpack he must have left under the sink while attending to her yesterday. Her cheeks burned, but she already knew what she was going to do. Sliding the lock closed on the door, she used the sink to help her kneel. She trembled slightly as she pinched the zip between her fingers, having second thoughts which were soon overpowered by her fingers unzipping the bag.

Inside was a small collection of clothes, and she pulled them out carefully, inhaling his scent. Other than those she only found toiletries near the bottom, he travelled light. She hadn't even realised his body wash was clutched in her hand until she'd clicked it open, allowing the fragrance to envelop her as she breathed it in, dabbing just a small amount on her wrist to keep the scent with her.

Just as she was putting things back, something else caught her eye. Crushed at the bottom of the bag was an envelope. Filled with curiosity, she removed it carefully, tracing the letters of her name on the beige paper with her finger, finding it impossible to swallow. Glancing towards the door, despite it being locked, she made sure no one was watching. With a shaking breath, she lifted the flap of the envelope. Gods, she remembered that smell, the scent of him mingled with ink and paper.

Jesse,

    I'm writing this on the train. I'm going to find you and place this in your hand, and if you still don't answer me, if you still can't reply, then I guess there's nothing left for us to say.

    All these years, I held on to the hope you were safe. I awaited a reply that never came and it killed me not knowing if you were alive.

    By the time I arrive, you'll already be married. I truly hope you're happy. Are you?

    I've made mistakes, I've done things I'm not proud of, things that can never be forgiven, but I love you and that's the one thing I have never regretted. You've always been the one for me, I know this, it's always been you. Only you.

I love you, Jesse Kyron, I always have, I always will, until the stars burn out and all life fades.

I know you don't feel the same, but can you find a way, some way, no matter how small, to keep me in your life since we'll be living in the same town? It would kill me if I had to see you, and you acted as if we were strangers. I know I failed you, that you owe me nothing, but can you find it in your heart to find even the smallest corner of your life for me?

Yours always,

A

Her hands shook as she returned the letter to the envelope, burying it back inside the bag, hiding all evidence of her invasion. She cupped her hands over her mouth, sobbing gently as Levi huddled close to her on the cold bathroom tiles. She stroked his short fur, holding him close.

Everything Alec said had been true, every word. He really had been writing, he really hadn't received her letters. Damn her father. Damn him to hell. All this time she'd thought he wasn't aware that Martha had smuggled her letters from the house. But where and when had the deception began? The pity in her maid's eyes as she kept saying she'd had no reply seemed so real. Had it too been an act?

Once she calmed, she tiptoed gingerly back into the room, certain she had heard him shuffle in the bed as the door unlocked, but as she looked upon him his eyes were closed. He looked peaceful. She reached out to touch his hair, to stroke the fringe from his eyes but, thinking better of disturbing him, she pulled back, folding the duvet over her as her skin grew cold.

Her body trembled until his arm encircled her again, sharing his heat. She snuggled back into his warmth, folding her arm over his to hold it close, savouring the feeling of being so safe in another's arms as she relaxed into the bond of comfort they had shared since childhood. It was a security she had seamlessly slipped back into. A safety she thought she would never feel again. Her eyelids drooped and, with a soft sigh, she sank back into slumber.

When next her eyes opened, it was daylight that streamed through the window, bathing the room in an illumination that had driven out all the remaining darkness. She moved slightly, her breath hitching as Alec's arm tightened protectively around her, drawing her closer to the warmth of his body. A blush chased across her cheek as he held her close, clearly dreaming of whatever girl he must have left behind. His rhythmic breathing teased the hairs around her ears, but the rough scratching of his stubble had gone.

"Rise and shine, Fae" he whispered into her hair, startling her. A smile tugged her lips at the sound of a name she hadn't heard for so long. He had said it fit her because she was always flitting around, busy and causing mischief. She rolled towards him, their noses almost touching as she gazed into his honey-coloured eyes. She lifted her chin, kissing his nose before she'd even realised what she'd done. Heat flushed across skin as she turned away, but a smile still traced her lips.

As she sat up, she noticed he was partially dressed, his perfectly fitting black jeans showing hints of the muscular thighs they hugged. She watched as he pulled a black shirt over his head, buttoning it slowly with the fingers that had caressed her with such tenderness just the day before. A spray of water left his damp hair as he ruffled his hand through it, pushing it from his eyes. She must have slept through him showering. She couldn't remember when last she had slept so well, and her heart ached as she realised how easy it would be to get used to waking in his arms.

"Did you say this was a bed-and-breakfast?" she asked as her stomach grumbled lightly. Her vision scanned the room seeking Levi, but although he had been lying beside her last night, he was nowhere to be seen. She got the distinct impression he really didn't like Alec.

She had never seen him behave so grumpily before, especially since no one but her could see him.

"Yes, but it's lunchtime." He finished buttoning his shirt, his sculpted abs now completely concealed beneath the dark, tailored fabric. Hobbling towards the window, she parted the curtains further, seeing the truth in his words as the blazing light of the sun dazzled her from above.

They were in the second storey of a large converted house that looked down upon the street below. Already shoppers milled about, their bright clothing bathing the streets in a wash of weaving colours as they went about their business. She turned back towards him, her gaze lingering on the door, realising it must open into the upstairs hall, not outside as she had initially assumed. Realising this made her feel just a little more comfortable about staying. "Bed," he commanded. She gasped as he scooped her in his arms, laying her back down gently. "You need to stay off your feet for a few days."

"I can't stay here. I need to get moving before Micah's men find me."

"They'll not find you here."

"But—"

"No buts, Jess. You stay there until you're healed and rested then, and only then, will we leave. Now," he continued, tossing some stationery on to the bed, "write an inventory of everything you're going to need." A flush crept across her face as she recognised the paper as being the same as the note from inside his bag. His eyebrows lowered slightly as he watched her, and she couldn't help but wonder what was behind that look. A look that caused her stomach to burn.

CHAPTER 5

Alec let out a strained breath as he closed the door to the B&B behind him. The sun had decided to bless the day, while the strong wind worked at chasing away the scant wispy clouds that otherwise marred the perfect blue sky. He glanced down to the list —*Please, Alec, I need help*—He pressed his fingers into his eyelids for a second as his heart squeezed in his chest. When he looked again, the letters had rearranged into the list he had asked for, her handwriting the same. Still the same as the letter he had received begging him for help, telling him she needed him.

The longer he stayed with her, the more danger she would be in, but he owed it to her at least to make sure she was safe, that she had supplies.

He might work for her father, he might be enslaved, but at least he still had a wage. After all, that kind of slavery was outlawed, and familiars were meant to walk undetected.

Time was his ally at the moment, but in six days he was expected to report to his new position. Could six days be enough now he had found her, now he knew that she had never forgotten him? No, eternity would not be sufficient. How could he ever bear to let her go again?

He rubbed his chest with the heel of his hand as the familiar ache returned. He had seen her do the same thing, her dainty hands raising, repeating the motion he himself was far too familiar with. He didn't know if he dared to hope that she felt their bond as strongly as he did.

He had been fourteen when he'd been forced to leave and, at that time, he had thought there was nothing that could compare to the way he felt for his first love, nothing stronger or more consuming than his obsession with the girl he would one day marry. The moment his eyes had fallen upon her again he had realised how wrong he had been. What he felt back then was a shadow of the feelings she stirred within him now.

The note crumpled in his hand. Six days would never be enough. Six days with her only to have leave her side again would destroy him anew. But there was no choice. He would take those days and the pain that would follow over never seeing her again. Every single time.

"Is that everything, sir?" The busty brunette batted her false eyelashes at him, leaning forward as she gave him the receipt. "Your sister really is lucky, I wish someone would buy me a new wardrobe." He glanced down at his bags, thinking that maybe he had gone a little overboard.

"The camping store on Marsh street, is it still open?"

"I've always enjoyed camping," she said, an obvious lie. People with such finely manicured nails, perfect hair and make-up rarely enjoyed roughing it outdoors. "Still going strong. Planning on a quiet getaway, are you?"

"Very quiet," he answered. Adjusting the bag handles he left the store, aware of her gaze following his every movement.

A loud thump at the door startled her. She froze for a breath before pushing herself off the bed, her hand reaching out to grab the bedside light, ripping the cord from the wall. A deep voice outside grumbled a curse that made panic course through her, her heart hammering in response to the building fear. They'd found her. Her hands trembled as she forced her breathing to calm. If they heard her movements, the game was over. She only had one chance.

She jumped as those outside banged again, two, three times in quick succession, though not as forceful as the first. Her feet screamed as she limped across towards the door. Levi was at her side, his ears pinned back, growling in the way only a cat could, a deep, reverberating howl. His posture tensed, teeth bared, hairs on end. This was not good. She watched him pounce through the wall, as if his presence would have an effect on whoever stood at the other side of the thin barrier. There had been times where Levi had fought with other shifter forms, which appeared to deplete the stamina of her attackers, so perhaps this was what he was doing now.

She still remembered the first time when Burnell, her father's right-hand man, had forced himself on her. As she fought, so too had Levi duelled to protect her honour. Burnell's boar essence had severely injured him, but their unseen combat had taken its toll on Burnell as well. Before this, she had never thought a shifter essence could be harmed.

Even when in play, other shifters' spirits never hurt one another. She believed it must have had something to do with the fact Levi was a spirit guardian since the same laws seemed not to apply. He could hurt them, but in turn they could also hurt him.

She had nursed Levi for days under the guidance of a young boy who was as much a spirit as Levi. She had scolded him, begging him through tear-filled eyes never to take such action again, never to leave her, but still he protected her the only way he could.

He had defended her every time her father raised his belt or flogger, every time Burnell crawled on top of her in the night. If not for him, she knew she would have suffered more and for longer. After, the two of them would lie together, united in their pain, and bring comfort to one another.

She released a shaky breath as the sound of metal rattled in the lock. She could hear it scraping, the grating sound like fingernails down a chalkboard. After they'd picked it, she'd have precious few seconds to deliver a stunning blow and hope whoever it was had come alone. Her grip tightened on the metal stand of the lamp, praying there was only one attacker, praying that the owner would know better than to allow a group of people entry without their being guests. They wouldn't want to draw too much attention. There had to be just one. It was her only hope, her only chance.

Stun him, slip past, run, hide.

She heard the lock release and fought back the urge to grasp the turning handle, pulling back her fingers that had been poised ready to grab it. The door opened inward, she'd never survive a battle of strength. Aim for the ear, she reminded herself, remembering one of the more devastating blows she landed on Burnell.

She saw her target, the dark hair, his back toward her as he pushed the door open, perhaps expecting her to flee. Without pause she swung, her gaze fixed upon her target. By the time she recognised the figure, and commonsense overwrote fear, the lamp was already in full momentum. He pivoted, dropping a handful of bags as he curled his arm, wrapping his hand around the back of his neck so his forearm absorbed the impact of the blow as he sheltered his head.

The glass lampshade shattered, sending shards of glass across the floor in a magnificent shower of reflected light and crystal. Alec's gaze snapped towards her as she stood panting, the lamp slipping from her trembling hands. She could feel her chest heaving as she stood frozen, unable to do anything but stare.

Without a word he dropped the remaining bags and scooped her in his arms, nudging the door closed with his heel carrying her to the bed. As he bent over her, she felt the heat rise to her cheeks. His scent was intoxicating, deliciously all-encompassing as her body shook from the adrenaline and she pulled in breath after breath, realising her nose was almost touching his, that she could feel his every exhalation on her face. She was inhaling the very air from his lungs, and somehow it was more fulfilling than any breath she had taken before.

"Alec..." she began. She had intended to apologise, but instead her voice came out breathy, her eyes dropping to his lips as she bit her own. She heard him groan slightly before pulling away, his eyebrows lowered as he levelled the same intense stare towards her that she had seen countless times before. No one had ever looked at her the way he did. It caused her stomach to burn in an unfamiliar way. She didn't know if she should be afraid of its intensity. But even had she wanted to be, his presence did nothing but soothe her.

"I'll clean up the glass." His shoulders heaved in a sigh as he turned his back towards her.

"Alec, I'm sorry. I thought..."

"Don't." A single word, firm, demanding, and she fell silent. It was a few moments before he spoke again. "Lunch." Another single word. He reached into a takeaway bag and at once the comfort of his scent was overpowered by the smell of food. He pulled something from another bag, his back towards her. As he turned, she saw he'd placed a burger on a paper plate. "Eat." He placed it beside her on the bed, watching her intently.

She wanted to talk, to apologise, but her stomach protested loudly. As she took a bite her eyes widened as she tasted the familiar explosion of flavours.

"You remembered." She opened the cheese burger to find a healthy dollop of peanut butter spread within, its gooey form already melting from the heat. He gave a chuckle, a low deep reverberating chuckle that made her toes curl as she smiled into the burger before taking another ravenous bite.

He placed the takeaway bag beside her, his thumb wiping a smudge of peanut butter from her lips. Her stomach warmed and the butterflies within began their dance as he placed it to his lips, sucking it while his gaze held her own. Her breath caught. Alec aged thirteen doing the very same thing had been the sexiest thing she had ever seen in her life. Until now.

This was beyond sexy. It was on a whole other level and she could do nothing but stare long after he had moved away. But this morning's passing thought of a girlfriend returned, along with the words she'd read in the letter. Her smile faded. "Alec?" she began, dropping her gaze towards the bedding. She studied the intricate pattern, how beige, red, and cream had been woven into delicate designs on the silken duvet.

"Just say it." She forgot he knew her tells, that he had always read her with ease.

"It's not that I don't appreciate all this, I do, really. But if you didn't come because I wrote, what are you doing here? Surely someone's waiting for you back home?" As much as she wanted to, she couldn't play make believe any more, pretend that he was hers, that he had come to save her. It was too dangerous.

When she was younger, he had told her he would marry her one day. It was a memory that had kept her going through some troubling times, but it had been make-believe, nothing more. His touch was too intimate, too addictive to become lost in if he wasn't going to stay.

Her mind raced back to the gentle way he'd washed her hair, the sensual rub that was both agonising and pleasurable. She bit her lower lip thinking about the times over the last day when she thought he was about to kiss her, when he would lean in close, teasing her as he brushed her hair behind her ears, and the way he caused her heart to race in an unfamiliar way. She couldn't do this, not if he was going to leave her again.

"I..." The sparkle of amusement in his eyes died, and for a moment he seemed at a loss for words. "I came here for work."

"Won't your employer be missing you?"

"They know how to reach me." He gave a nonchalant shrug as he turned away, but there was something in his tone, a weight to his words that made her worry. She gingerly stood, placing her hand lightly to his shoulder, encouraging him to turn back towards her, to look at her.

His eyes were smouldering as he caressed her jaw softly with his knuckles in a way that made her shudder. She had never thought there to be anything intimate about that part of a person's body. She had thought they could only bring pain. She only hoped she would never feel the sting of his touch, even kindness could bring pain. Her father had played with her in such ways for a long time, sending someone to her to pretend to care, to gain her trust, only for that person to betray her. It was one of his games, one of the ways he had sought to break her.

She knew better than to let herself be vulnerable, but there was an intimacy to the gesture that made her heart sing, as if any moment he would lower his head and kiss her. She closed her eyes in anticipation as he moved a little closer. His lips brushed her cheek as he buried his face into her hair by her ear. "Let's get you into something more suitable for a lady of such fair beauty," he whispered in a husky voice that made her heart quicken. Turning, she pressed her lips to his before he had a chance to pull away, before she could change her mind.

The feeling of his soft lips on hers somehow released every wall she had ever created, unleashing a torrent of emotions she had dared not feel for longer than she could imagine. For years she had pushed everything away—her pain, her heartache, herself—and his lips, with a single touch, undid her. His hands pressed against her gently, easing her away.

'*Idiot.*' Closing her eyes for but a moment, she cursed herself silently.

"Jess, I—" But his rejection stilled, his eyes gravitating towards hers, searching her face before his head lowered to claim her lips possessively.

She moaned into his mouth as he exposed her soul, shattering every boundary she'd ever created. His hand dropped from her face, skimming her breast lightly before grasping her waist, pulling her towards him with a need as desperate as her own while his other wove into her hair, holding her close, keeping her next to him.

A gentle gasp escaped her kiss-swollen lips as he pulled back slightly, his breath so warm on her sensitive skin as he trailed butterfly-soft kisses down her neck towards her collar bone. His desperate, anguished groans heated her stomach as he pulled her closer, guiding her closer towards the bed, causing goose-pimples to chase across her flesh.

She clung on to him desperately, needing his warmth, savouring his touch as she let her head fall backwards, extending her neck as he began to release the buttons of the shirt she wore. She wanted him to kiss every inch of her, to feel his hand erasing every touch that ever came before as only he could do. She wanted him, needed him.

She felt the dampness on her cheeks as her every breath began to tremble as intensely as her body. A coldness enveloped her as he pulled away. His warmth vanished, leaving her chilled, daring a look she saw his gaze focused on her newest imperfection.

'Idiot,' she cursed herself again. Of course he wouldn't want her, ache for her as she did him. She was damaged, scarred, broken, ugly. Why had she even thought he could be interested? 'Idiot.' She reached out, grasping the blanket duvet from the bed, wrapping it around herself, covering her imperfections as a look of annoyance flashed through his eyes.

"Jess." He grasped her waist, kissing her lightly once more as he pushed the duvet from her shoulders. "I will be your shield. From this day I will protect you always." There was a power to his words that caused her to shiver at his raw and honest vow.

But she didn't want protecting, she wanted him to love her.

She wanted him to take her in his arms and breathe new life into her, but now he could barely even meet her gaze. How could he say such things and then look away, could he not see how badly she needed him? Her heart seemed to stall for a second as he gathered the scattered bags from the floor.

"About paying you back," she prompted, keeping her voice light, trying not to think, to feel. Never had anyone kissed her like that before. Never had she so desperately wanted to be kissed again. He had disarmed her, unlocked everything she had kept sealed within herself, and now she would force it back to where it belonged. "I only have," she said, opening the expensive leather wallet and placing her finger over a picture of herself as she studied the collection of notes inside, wondering how deep Micah's obsession ran if he was already carrying her photo, "this much."

"I have it covered." He placed the bags on the bed alongside a hiker's backpack before stepping into the bathroom and locking the door behind him. A moment later, she heard the shower and, pushing down the feeling of rejection, decided to look at what he had brought.

Alec let the cold water of the shower wash over him. This was killing him. *She* was killing him. The way he felt complete, whole, within her presence was almost too much. It was as if the past fourteen years had never happened, as though they had never been apart.

Gods, he loved her. He loved her so much his chest ached. He hadn't expected her to kiss him, and certainly hadn't meant to kiss her back. It had taken every ounce of his resolve not to lift her in his arms and carry her to the bed, to show her the true depth of his love, and bury himself inside her.

He wanted nothing more than to hear her scream his name, to exhaust her completely and lie with his skin pressed so tightly against hers that he could no longer tell where he ended and she began. Because in a way he couldn't. He was incomplete without her, broken and hollow.

He had been such an idiot. Her lips had been an obsession, her taste a drug, and he had needed more, wanted more. His hands had roamed across her body as he ached to be near her. There had been just her, the addiction of her scent, her touch, and he had lost every inhibition as he sought finally to claim every inch of her as his own.

He hadn't even realised what he was doing until he heard her soft crying and felt her trembling beneath his touch.

'What was I thinking?' he scolded himself silently. The last thing he wanted was for her to feel unsafe, that he was expecting something more from her than she was ready to give. He had seen her scars, Burnell's mark upon her. He could only imagine what she had suffered, and yet the fool that he was had been unable to rein in his desire. He'd made her cry.

Damn it, he'd made her cry.

He rested his head against the tiled wall. It wasn't fair. He couldn't do this to himself, to her, especially since ultimately he would betray her. It would be better if he kept his distance. He wanted to tell her everything, but he couldn't, the one thing he could never do since he was forced to take the oath of blood and magic, was tell anyone what he was, and it was this very thing that made him as dangerous to her as any who sought her.

His fist connected with the wall as he swore under his breath.

She was his soulmate, the very air that gave him life. It shouldn't be so difficult.

CHAPTER 6

Hearing the shower stop, Jesse quickly hid beneath the covers, covering herself completely until only her face could be seen peeking out from beneath the heavy duvet. She heard his footsteps freeze as the door opened and felt the weight of his stare upon her. She kept her eyes closed, hoping, praying, he'd think she was asleep.

His bare feet padded across the wooden flooring until the mattress behind her dipped under his weight. He snuggled close, stroking her hair as he lay beside her.

"I'm so sorry," he murmured, and she could tell from his whisper-soft tones he thought she was asleep. His voice was so quiet even she strained to hear it. She focused on her breathing, trying not to betray her act. "I've waited fourteen years to hold you. I didn't mean to push you. I will wait as long as you need me to, and if you're never ready, that's okay, too. What you suffered because I couldn't keep my promise..." He sighed softly, an exhale filled with such pain and remorse her chest began to ache again. "I'm so sorry, Jess, I never meant to make you cry. I never meant for you to feel anything but safe with me. I hope you can forgive me. I love you, Jesse Kyron, until the stars burn out and all life fades, and nothing will ever change that." He wrapped his arm around her, tensing as she turned towards him. For a moment she just stared into his eyes and saw it all, the pain, the love, the regret.

"You idiot," she whispered through her tears, her lips seeking his. She kissed him desperately, as if he was a breath of air and she was suffocating, as if he were water and she was dying in a vast desert, because without him she had been, without him she couldn't breathe and from the day he left until he had taken her in his arms she hadn't lived.

Her stomach burned as he groaned into her mouth. She could feel his need, and it was every bit as consuming as her own. His lips crushed against hers and, for a moment, there was nothing in the world but their desperation, the urgency of their love. She pulled him on top of her, her desire-filled eyes begging him as her hand slid down his tense muscles to his trousers, her trembling fingers fighting against the buttons.

"Jess." The husky growl of his voice caused her to shiver. He pulled away, only for her hands to weave within his hair, pulling him back to her, refusing to let him go. She ached to be near him, a yearning beyond anything she had felt before. Without his touch she felt empty, dead. She wanted to feel alive, to live.

Every kiss, every touch, breathed life into her soul, revived everything she had lost, everything the years of abuse had stripped from her. She wanted him, she needed him.

"Please," she whispered as he pulled away again. She saw his Adam's apple rise and fall, his intense gaze causing her to melt as her stomach continued to burn. His desire consumed her, breathed life into her, and all she wanted, all she needed, was him.

"Are you sure?" His eyes rolled backwards, his breathing shuddered as she tugged his trousers down over his hips.

"Please, Alec," she begged again, aware of the desire coating her voice. His lips sought hers again, returning her need, her desperation.

"Then allow me to show you how beautiful you truly are," his husky voice growled.

Jesse awoke still tangled within Alec's arms, her muscles burning. She took a moment to appreciate the way the sunlight caused his stubble to shimmer in different colours, different shades of browns and reds. His heavy lashes were closed. He looked so innocent in his sleep, not at all like the ferocious lover she had lost herself to the last days. Even remembering the way his intense gaze smouldered as he looked upon her caused her pulse to race.

She had never realised sex could be like that.

He had explored every inch of her hungrily, until she could take no more, making her scream and beg for him. He had made love to her slowly. It was sensual, erotic, something more than she had ever felt, far more than an act of disgrace that left her feeling humiliated and ashamed. Tears had slipped from her eyes without control.

He hadn't just fucked her as Burnell had, he hadn't used her body, he had worshipped every inch of her, making her feel things she never realised were possible.

For one moment she had seen Alec's regret as he took her in his arms. A moment of insecurity and doubt that had made her heart swell even more. She had been so overwhelmed, it had taken her far too long to explain, far too long to assure him it wasn't regret or pain behind her tears, but something she couldn't even voice. A feeling of being so completely loved.

She stroked her hand across his bare chest, appreciating the ripple of every sculpted muscle. They had spent the last two days discovering every inch of each other and, for but a moment, she had forgotten the world outside, the life she had once lived. For but a moment her life had been everything she had once fantasised about, only so much better, because it had not been a dream and she had lived and experienced each and every toe-curling moment of it.

Today, however, things were going to change. They were up and dressed shortly before dawn. Alec was already glancing through the curtains with a look of concern knitted across his brow.

Last night, when he had returned with supper, he had told her it was time to move on. It was too soon to risk the railway station. Her timing for the train had to be perfect, timed to coincide with the busiest traffic in the hope she could slip by unseen but, until then, they needed somewhere safe to hide. He hadn't elaborated on what he had seen, but the way he was constantly checking outside had told her everything she'd needed to know. Her stomach had become a pit of anxiety ever since, reality had once more found its way to infiltrate her dreams.

Last night he had hidden her honey-hair beneath a brown toner, his attentive fingers no longer taking her back to memories of her childhood, but keeping her in the moment, savouring his every touch. At a glance he thought she was different enough not to ring any instant alarm bells, something further enhanced by the overly large, fashionable sunglasses he'd brought her. She still remembered the sound of his laughter as she'd wrapped one of the scarves he'd bought her to conceal the collar around her hair, pulling the glasses to the tip of her nose to imitate an actress from one of the old movies they had watched together as children.

With his assistance, disappearing into obscurity shouldn't be too difficult. The collar could be concealed, and it helped that her father had ensured she had not been chipped. While it had been done as a means of controlling her, it was now a blessing. Had she been, like Alec and a large number of the people living in Mython, then Micah would have already found her. Of course, it also meant she had no access to any funds except for the small amount in the stolen wallet.

Alec shivered beneath her touch, a smile on his lips as he lay watching her, clearly savouring the moment as much as she was. She wondered if he would be leaving, too. He had spoken of his plan for her to leave last night as he wrapped her feet for what would be the last time, thanks to the enchanted bandages and her own accelerated healing. What he hadn't mentioned was if he would be standing beside her when the time came for her to leave.

"Do you have everything you need?" Alec questioned, tracing his hand down her hips, teasing a soft moan from her lips.

"Not quite everything," she whispered, drawing him in for a kiss.

Alec watched as Jesse gathered her things into the bag he had purchased, a frown creasing his brow. Something she had said a few days ago was still bothering him. As he had lay holding her, she asked about why he had left so suddenly. The truth was, he hadn't known about being sent to study until the day he was told he was leaving. Their goodbye had been shorter than he had wanted, but she sensed more behind her question.

It had been difficult to keep his answers vague. If she didn't remember what he was to their family, he felt no need to shame himself by telling her. Not that he could announce his position. He could never tell anyone he was a familiar, the words just wouldn't come.

His schooling had consisted of three parts. The everyday military officer training school, the segregated lessons about his roles and responsibilities, and, when he was old enough, the tasks her father would have him undertake, from securing loyalties to silencing leaks.

It was a little-known secret that his master had aligned with the vampires, helping them conceal the spread of their sleepers through the guise of a new illness, Pyrexia Blight. Lord Kyron's contacts were vast, ensuring no one thought anything was amiss when the blood-work returned with a new strain of virus. It had been the perfect ploy.

These new Atelís wouldn't be what anyone expected. They weren't just sleeping vampires awaiting to be awakened. They were something new, an army that, when awakened, would be subservient to the lords who were responsible for their creation. That was why there were no bite tags or signs of pending preternatural transformation in those afflicted. When the time came, and all the pieces were in place, those opposing the council would awaken their masses and go to war.

The virus was spreading quickly since the clan leaders behind the movement used every opportunity to swell their ranks. There was only one place whose statistics were not on par with the movement. Overton. One of his more recent missions had been to speak to Vincent Masters and discover why his territory was behind schedule. But, as it turned out, this ancient vampire had been brought to justice by the Preternatural Task Force—aka the P.T.F.—months before he had arrived.

Fortunately for Lord Kyron and his allies, his investigation showed their interest in him had solely been related to his extracurricular activities, namely the acquisition and trading of Tabus, rather than the other more incriminating engagements. He had, however, been unable to ascertain the reason for their lack of numbers.

Devon, one of Vincent Master's trusted men, had assured him personally that the targets were being infected but, to their confusion, were showing signs of recovery, and their blood work had confirmed that the PB virus had been eliminated from their system. The only possibility he could conceive was that the territory had somehow received a faulty batch of mutagens, something he had recently reported.

Lord Kyron, however, was concerned that there was more to this situation, a saboteur or a traitor in the ranks, and it had been this report that had triggered his return. It seemed Lord Kyron was not as convinced about the innocence of this development as everyone else was, and he wanted his bodyguard nearby.

Alec ran his hands through his brown hair, pushing his fringe from his eyes as they gravitated towards the metal band still secured around Jesse's neck while she wrapped a silver chiffon scarf around to conceal it. He smiled inwardly at her attempt to wrap it. Standing, he untangled the mess and took its ends in his hands, pulling her towards him for a soft kiss as he retied it the way the woman in the store had demonstrated, although his version barely resembled the elegant wrap he had seen, he somehow managed to make it look stylish. He stepped back, admiring his work with a grin, appreciating how the silver colour drew attention to her blue eyes.

Three days. Only three days remained until he had to leave and he had still not found a way to remove that accursed suppressor from around her neck, so the scarf had been the only solution he could think of. At the collar's rear were two almost rounded areas he recognised were intended for thumbs. He had tried to pry them apart, but he was certain it could be unlocked only by the person it belonged to. Micah.

Unable to remove it, he had helped the only other way he knew how, by ensuring Jesse would have enough money to start a new life. She could have a fresh start. The only thing he had not told her was that it had to be without him. When their time together ended, for her own safety, she could never contact him again.

Three days, in just three days he would watch her walk away, taking with her everything he was.

He had sworn to himself he wouldn't do this, he wouldn't pursue her this way, or let himself fall in love with her all over again. He had known how dangerous it would be, how impossible their relationship was, and still he had been unable to resist. Even knowing that watching her leave would destroy him, he had still been unable to stop himself.

For one moment, for seven short days, he would live the life he had only dreamt about and then he would have to let go. But he didn't know if he could. In just four days she had taken his darkness, everything tainted and corrupted about him, and filled it with her light. They had healed each other, and to let her go would destroy him. But there was no choice. He needed her safe.

The number of suits searching the town had increased, along with others he had spotted who were not quite so obvious in their intentions. It was only a matter of time until they found her. Fortunately, he knew just the place she could hide.

He zipped the train ticket dated for Saturday back into the side pocket of her bag. It was the best time for her to slip away. The approaching festival would see an influx of visitors disembarking, providing cover and camouflage for her to steal aboard the train and slip away from this town, from him. He had brought an open-ended ticket, so she could get off the train anywhere she felt like and continue the journey later if necessary. It was better for everyone that he didn't know where she was.

Thinking of his tasks brought his focus back to Jesse. Her father had no idea they were together, and he wondered how he could ensure this remained the case. For now, he would enjoy his freedom, enjoy the feeling of completion in her presence and use what little time he had left to ensure she reached somewhere safe, somewhere no one, not even he, would find her.

He sat on the edge of the bed, his mind awash with weighted thoughts. Their time together had been more than he had ever expected to have, moments that were his alone and shared with the woman he had loved and adored his entire life.

Their kiss had been his undoing, a sweet promise, a temptation of a life he knew could never be his. After her lips had found his, he felt the need to bare his heart, to tell her how he was bound in service. But no matter how much he wanted to tell her everything, he couldn't. Instead, he surrendered to the desire that had been building since her first butterfly kiss, a kiss that had ruined him.

No other woman had even come close to holding a candle to how he felt about her, despite how hard he'd tried to move on. She was his soulmate, both he and her mother had known it, and from the way she kissed him, from the way her body had responded to his every touch, he was certain she knew, too.

He had recognised Burnell's distinctive pattern of scarring on her flesh, a wound he left on all his unwilling conquests. The fact she had been so ready to accept him not only sang of their bond, but of her strength. As she cried after he had claimed her for his own, he had cursed himself, certain she hadn't been ready, that he had given into his own needs without thinking of what was right for her. But as he held her, apologising, she had brushed away his fears. No one had made love to her before, made her feel the way he had. She told him he had wiped the corruption from her soul before kissing him again with such passion that he had no choice but to show her once more the depth of his love and how two people in love should really be joined.

"I'm ready." She touched his knee as she sat beside him. "Penny for your thoughts."

"Just going over the plan. We need to move, to lie low for a few days. It means a long walk, but I know a place you should be safe. It's not much, but I also think it'll be the last place anyone looks for you. How do you feel about heights?"

Jesse was well aware her mouth was hanging agape as she looked up towards the tree house. The structure seemed old. Moss had stained the walls that were bathed in perpetual shadow, creating a dark green hue to the wooden construction. The thatched roof looked weathered and bowed ever so slightly as if long overburdened, telling tales of years of neglect,.

Her fingers traced around the edge of the silver choker, her finger curling around it to give it another futile tug. Normally she could see the dryads playing and the sylph chasing currents on the wind.

Her sight had been filled with visions of wonder and the movement of magic through all living things. Everything incorporeal had been hers to behold, everything. Now there was nothing. Her eyes no longer beheld the wonders she had once taken for granted. She allowed her gaze to stray towards Alec, a smile lifting her lips. She wouldn't change a thing, she would give it up all over again to see him. While Micah's collar had plunged her world into something mundane, with Alec beside her she had all the colours and vibrancy she could ask for.

Alec had tried everything he could think of to remove the burden, from bolt cutters to runic enchantments purchased on parchment and empowered by a local witch, but eventually he had needed to admit the futility of his efforts. Such a contraption, by design, could be released only by the person it was attuned to. And there was no chance she would let Micah get close enough to remove it. She had asked Alec how he had known what it was when she hadn't told him of its effects, but his only answer had been the racing of her own pulse as he grasped the back of her neck, pulling her in towards his lips for another rejuvenating breath of life.

Figment whispers scratched and scraped for her ears alone as Levi's enormous paws found purchase against the trunk to pull himself high into the branches above. Just moments before he navigated the platform, he cast a downward glance, his snort still audible as his gaze fell on Alec.

Jesse smiled to herself. He had made abundantly clear by his absence over the last few days he did not approve of Alec. He wasn't used to sharing her affections, but surely, once he saw how happy he made her, how kind and gentle he was, the animosity would fade. She had never heard him growl and hiss as much as he did when he and Alec were in the same area, nor had she ever felt the sting of his absence so much. Despite Alec's arms being around her at night, Levi would still snuggle close, his tail swishing in annoyance. He was cross with her, but still came to her hand for affection when Alec wasn't around.

Her gaze strayed to Alec, offering him a reassuring smile. Even though she knew he was quite unaware of Levi's existence, she was certain she couldn't be the only one to feel the increase in air pressure when the two of them shared a space together.

A slight tugging sensation in her mind told her Levi thought the area above to be safe. He appeared a moment later to glance dismissively down towards them again before tiptoeing across one of the tree boughs. His claws sunk into the bark, leaving phantom etches upon its surface, before lounging across it, throwing one final look of disgust towards Alec. Biting her lower lip, she held back her amusement. Never before had she seen a cat look so annoyed.

"How do you even know about this place?" she asked, her hand on the warm bark of the gnarled old trunk as she circled the thick base. Her fingers found signs of a long-forgotten engraving, perhaps a declaration of love or friendship. Her gaze drifted across it, hoping to decipher the long forgotten code, but the moss and fungi now coating this ancient surface made it impossible.

"Your mother." She felt her lips part slightly at his answer. She must have frozen because the next thing she knew he was behind her, his hands grasping her hips, pulling her close. "Here, look." He took her hand in his, extending it towards the markings she had been studying. She glanced over her shoulder at him, feeling suddenly shy as he traced her fingers over the initials: AB & MB. "She brought me here a few days before…" His expression held the weight of things better left unsaid, and after their long walk she felt too tired push for further answers. "How much do you remember about her?" He stroked her cheek with his knuckles in a way that made it hard to swallow as she glanced up at him. The sun piercing through the canopy bathed him it its warm embrace making his honey eyes glow with more than just the desire with which he beheld her.

"Not much. I remember how she used to wash my hair and sing songs, and dance." She smiled sadly, "I remember her placing my hand in yours and dancing. But mostly my memories of her are just vague impressions. The only image I have of any clarity is the one I wish I could forget, and yet part of me is glad I can't because as long as I relive that night I'll never truly forget her. That must sound strange."

Her mother's last breaths were seared into her mind, the way her slender fingers had clawed at her father's hands as he slid her lithe frame up the wall, holding her there, choking the life from her. She could still recall the desperate scuffling sound of her mother's bare feet against the wall, the way her hair—the same colour as her own—had been braided ready for sleep.

Her nightgown had been like something from one of the old movies they used to watch together, cream and so long her feet had kept scraping against it as she fought. She had watched helplessly from the landing as her mother's beautiful face twisted while her father crushed the life from her body, slowly, as if he had savoured each second of her final struggle.

She was only thankful her legs had found the strength to move before her father had ascended the stairs and secured a noose around her bruised neck, and that she didn't witness him hauling her mother over the landing for the servants to find hanging in the morning. No one even questioned if it had really been suicide, despite the clear prints upon her throat.

"Not at all." His gaze studied her for a moment, and something akin to guilt briefly shadowed his eyes. "Do you think you can climb?" He pointed to the notches on the tree. Her brow furrowed as she realised while not one of them had been carved, each had been perfectly crafted, as if the tree had grown those knots and crevices just to provide access to the structure above.

With a nod, she reached up, amazed at how far the first foothold was from the ground. Alec followed behind, occasionally placing his hand to her ass when her balance seemed to waver, although she wasn't certain if she faltered because of her exhaustion or his touch. As she reached the top, she raised her hand, as if instinctively knowing there was a trapdoor. In spite of the years of dirt and debris sealing evidence of the opening, it moved with ease, although the tattered remains of the fraying rope used to lift it from above had seen better days.

What remained of the tree house door lay in tatters. The soft wooden panels had long succumbed to the elements and crumpled in on a pile of decaying leaves and debris, some of which still held the russet tones of autumn, despite summer's heat beating down from above.

Looking across from the platform, the forest still held a unique magic. While she no longer saw the beings who called this place their home, the way the dappled light caught the pollen within its pale green beams created a scene of magic all of its own. Closing her eyes, she listened to the rustle of the heavily burdened branches. The green leaves below, that helped to disguise this small dwelling, whispered a greeting and she found in its voice a peace second only to being held in Alec's embrace.

A sudden jolt made her squeal as he swept her from her feet, spinning her around before carrying her over the threshold. His lips crashed against hers with an urgency and desperation that never seemed to fade no matter how many times he claimed her lips as his own. His hand slid beneath her top, she tensed for but a second as his rough fingertips caressed her scars before laying her on the floor. The leaves created a soft and earthy blanket that mingled with his spicy scent as she wrapped her legs around him, refusing to let him pull away. Her fingernails left thick crevices in the soft bark that scratched against her back as he deepened his kisses. She placed her hand to his face, leaving a trail of dirt upon his flushed skin.

"You're killing me, Jess," he groaned as he planted another soft kiss upon her neck. "Work first." He pulled away, grasping her hand, pulling her to her feet in a smooth and fluid motion. Licking her lips, she savoured his taste for a moment longer, but as she looked around, she realised he was right. They couldn't stay here in its current condition, but it was nothing a quick tidy couldn't resolve.

The structure, including the floor, had been built from large trunks, levelled out by fixing carefully sculpted inserts between the curves as best as possible to create an uneven but natural floor. The inside lacked the green hue of the outside, and had been varnished in a deep mahogany stain, causing the grey stone wall of the far wall to stand out. Her eyes studied it intently, observing the cast-iron pot suspended above the hearth, while her mind conjured images of stray sparks burning the structure to ashes.

Alec pressed a besom he had pulled from the cobwebbed corner into her hand.

"You sweep, I'll—"

"Oh?" She raised an eyebrow teasingly. "Because I'm a woman I have to clean?"

"That's right, wench." He grinned, playfully smacking her backside. His face grew serious, and she saw his amusement fade. She placed her lips to his, reassuring him in the best way possible his gesture didn't require any overthinking. She held him close, her fingers stroking the coarse hairs of his five o'clock shadow.

"And what will my strong hunter-gatherer be doing while this woman folk attends to this?" she whispered, nibbling on his ear. His spicy scent of cinnamon and ginger conjured images of huddling down against the winter snow and cold nights that were still so many seasons away.

"Gathering firewood for dinner. How else will my woman cook lunch for me?" She grinned, her stomach burning in response to the way he called her his woman.

"Well, this woman hopes her man has a stomach made from the same iron as his abs if he plans to eat her cooking." She rubbed her hand across his torso, her fingers tracing his defined muscles. She'd never actually learnt to cook, but was hoping it wouldn't be too hard, although she had a sneaking suspicion she could feed him leaves and bugs and he'd still eat it with a smile. An iron stomach wouldn't be too bad a thing for him to have at all.

"Behave," he cautioned. "I shouldn't be too long, then I'll be back to help with this. There are snacks and water in my bag." He kissed her forehead before making his way to the collapsed door. "Promise me you won't leave."

"I'll be waiting." She stroked her hand down his face, already missing him even though he had not yet left.

After watching him disappear into the forest, Jesse returned inside to take stock. Aside from the ash and cobweb-filled hearth, there were a few makeshift cupboards with warped doors hanging precariously on rusted hinges. A small table and two chairs were stacked in the corner. The way they seemed to lean against the wall told her she knew better than to trust her weight to them. Sunlight from one of the two windows streamed through small rain-cleaned patches of dirt-encrusted glass to draw her focus towards the clump of rotting rags and sheets bundled beneath.

Grasping the besom from where she'd set it, she dusted the cobwebs aside. Thick plumes of dust rose, assailing her nose and throat until the sound of her coughs filled the air. Dashing to the wooden windows, she pushed them open, cringing as one of the small squares of glass slid from the crumbling wooden partition. Placing her scarf over her mouth, she began to sweep again, thankful the wind had picked up to chase the gritty dust clouds away.

The clattering sound of the table and chair collapsing as her besom barely ticked their legs made her shriek. With hands on her hips, she studied the soft, splintered heap before placing the wood into the cleaned hearth, trying not to think about why Alec was taking so long.

By the time she had finished, the small tree house looked almost habitable. Almost. Grabbing a T-shirt from her bag, she doused it in a small amount of the bottled water and began wiping the inside of the pot from the hearth, thankful that the lid had spared it the same weathering as the rest of the house. With that done, she wiped down the area beneath the window where they would sleep. Despite being brushed, the floor was still thick with dirt, turning the white shirt black.

She hadn't realised exactly how much time had passed until the birds' evening chorus echoed, making her cast her gaze outside where she noticed the dusky hue of the sky. The intense shades of purples and blues above gave the promise of a starry night. Though Mython was sealed behind a barrier that kept it sheltered from the rest of the world, the stars always seemed impossibly bright. Her stomach tightened as her thoughts returned to Alec's absence.

Trying to push the disquiet from her mind, she dribbled a little more water on to the floor, using the filthy garment to wipe down the area where they would sleep once more. As the sky grew black overhead, she pulled one of the blankets from the camping bag, wedging it between small splits in the wood to hang loosely over the door.

Her skin prickled as she worried about what had happened to Alec. He would be back, after all, he'd told her to wait for him. Sensing her growing distress, Levi brushed against her thigh. He had only been gathering firewood. How could he be missing for the best part of the day? Her fingers twisted the ends of her scarf. Clearly something had delayed him, perhaps a danger he hadn't wanted to follow him here.

She lay on the remaining blanket, forcing her eyes to close, tossing and turning as dreams of Alec lying injured haunted her sleep. She heard Levi purring beside her and wrapped her arm around him, drawing comfort from his presence.

CHAPTER 7

Alec stood silently before Lord Kyron, eyes lowered, hands clasped behind his back. The only thing he was grateful for was that he hadn't been with Jesse when he had been summoned. Until that one moment he had been certain he could fight the familiar compulsion, but no sooner had the tug upon his soul come, the firewood had dropped from his arms and his body betrayed him.

It was impossible to describe the feeling. He was still present, aware, but without control. He felt as if he had been torn in two, part of him needing to obey while another part clawed desperately to defy. Everything Lord Kyron had asked of him he had done without question, but this was different, he needed to protect Jesse.

"Did you really think I wouldn't know you were with her? I knew you'd find her, that's why I brought you back when I did." Alec didn't flinch, but inside he was reeling. Lord Kyron knew where Jesse was, he knew, and Alec had no way of warning her. All he could do was stand and listen, just as he had been ordered to. "It just so happens your reunion was part of my plan. I can't wait until she sees what I have in store. Tell me, how was your time with my daughter? I want to hear everything."

'*No!*' His thoughts protested. But he didn't even manage to bite his lip. Instead, every detail fell from his traitorous mouth, from the moment he first saw her at the railway station to leaving her in the forest.

He had tried to swallow every word, to withhold one detail, no matter how small, but he simply stood there, betraying her as he always feared he would. He'd thought he still had three days, three days to get her to safety, three days until he could genuinely claim, if asked, he had no idea where she was. Damn it, he'd waited too long and now she was going to pay the price of his mistake.

"Worry not. You will be reunited soon enough. You are not to leave this property or speak a word to my daughter unless otherwise instructed. Is that clear?"

'*No, no fucking way,*' he screamed silently while his own voice echoed back, "Yes, Master, your will be done"

"Indeed it will. If you're a good soldier, maybe I'll even let you play with her once I've bound her as my newest familiar." The words struck him harder than any physical blow could have ever done, stripping all the colour from his world as he heard this declaration. Yet despite the vice-like grasp crushing his soul, his treacherous heart continued to beat, his lungs continued to breathe.

He couldn't let this happen. There had to be something he could do, something, anything. She couldn't be bound like him, she deserved better than that, better than his existence. He should have put her on the train instead of selfishly revelling in her presence, instead of waiting for her wounds to heal. If he'd only sent her away the day they'd been reunited, she'd be safe, but the thought of spending time with her, of holding her, had been too much to deny himself, and Lord Kyron had known, he'd known he would find her. Damn it. He had played into his hands without so much of a whispered request. "Dismissed."

Alec's feet carried him from the small audience room. The moment the door closed behind him the tension holding him released, causing him to stagger a few paces as his breathing finally caught up to the panic coursing through his veins. His hand pressed against the textured wallpaper while his other massaged his chest.

"She's a good lay." Alec bristled at the sound of that voice. Burnell. He stood with his back resting against the wall, near the door from which he had just emerged. His broad frame and ample girth made the thick wooden door appear small in his presence, and the great hallway seem too narrow. His lips twisted into a smirk as he moved towards Alec and through his greyscale world, Alec saw red.

The memory of his mark marring Jesse's skin pierced his mind with white-hot rage caused his fists to clench without conscious thought. He wanted to kill him, to wipe that arrogant smile off his face, to drive his fist repeatedly through his skull, breaking his every bone until not even his mother would have recognised the mangled mass of blubber and pulp that remained. He turned sharply, ready to follow through on his desire, but his arm betrayed him.

Mirth lit Burnell's features as he saw him struggle, his intention clear. "Though," he continued, leaning down to place his lips near Alec's ear, "I like it better when she fights. The sound of her screaming as she writhes beneath me, kicking and bucking as I repeatedly drive my cock into her tight pussy is second to none. You'll see," he goaded, slapping Alec's shoulder.

"I'll never hurt her and you'd better keep your hands to yourself," Alec warned, already knowing it was an empty threat. Burnell knew he couldn't raise a hand against him. He couldn't hurt anyone in his master's employ.

"Or what?" he taunted with a knowing wink. "Go on, *familiar*, try it, I dare you. I can't wait until she's back where she belongs. My cock is craving some sweet action."

"Don't. You. Dare." His nails were digging so hard into his palms he could feel the skin beneath them part, mingling sweat with blood as he tried against all hope to defend her honour, to bring her the justice she deserved.

"Who's going to stop me? Certainly not you. Maybe I'll let you watch, let you see how a real man takes a whore."

Alec felt his world implode. For fourteen years he had lived without her. Fourteen years. He should have just stayed away. Lord Kyron had known everything, of that he was certain. He must have seen the letters, understood how neither he nor Jesse could let the other go. He had used their connection, just as Jesse's mother, Adeline, had always feared he would. There had to be something he could do, a way to protect her.

His heart hammered in his chest, its every beat morphing to accusations. *Traitor, traitor, traitor.* He had been bound by bloodline to this family, but the act of securing a new familiar was far more difficult than inheriting existing ties. They either had to submit willingly or be forced into submission.

She had suffered her father and Burnell for years, and still she fought his oppression with a strength that made him proud. He was certain even he would not have her resolve. It would take something momentous to force her into submission, to bend her to his will. The hallway shifted, sending the world around him spinning as an icy fear washed over him. Lord Kyron already had everything he needed. He only required one weapon. Him.

Micah had been watching Jesse since the report of her attempted abduction from the street. If only he had got there sooner she would be back where she belonged, back with him. He wasn't certain what Alec's game was, but it seemed he was trying to earn her trust.

For four days, he watched him come and go in the large house that had been converted into a respectable B&B many years ago. Once or twice he had even caught a glimpse of Jesse, parting the curtains with her finger to peek through, but he knew better than to approach the reception. They would never let an unexpected guest gain entry.

Micah kept a close tab on Alec from the moment he left the room, his most trusted people keeping him in sight as he called in the pharmacy, the women's clothing shops, even the camping store. They were there when he brought food and, for one foolish moment, as he watched him buy a train ticket, he had allowed himself to believe he was acting in her best interest. He just didn't realise her best interest was being returned to him.

The ticket booth operator confirmed the ticket was for the first Saturday train, but he wouldn't have expected anything less, not from someone with Alec's extensive military training. Utilising the camouflage of a crowd was far from a new technique, but even should he get her on the train, there would be people waiting, ready to apprehend her at the next station. Too many years had gone into this plan to let her slip through his fingers now. Her place was with him.

Three days ago, right on schedule, Alec had become suspicious, striking up conversations with those ordered to keep him in sight. It had unfolded exactly as he intended. After all, her father's men were looking for her too, and it would only be a matter of time before they found her.

Yesterday, he'd insisted Freya follow them as they slipped from the B&B just moments before the sun began to rise. The streets had been deserted, and she was the best at stalking. She had shifted into her cheetah, hiding in shadows and following them across the tree branches to a place they had no business being.

She had reported back everything, the way she had felt confident that Alec had meant Jesse no harm, how they seemed to be, as he had feared, in love. But love changed nothing. Just as the way he had left her in the middle of the woods, without protection, to return to his master had proven.

"Is that *familiar* still at Kyron's manor?" Micah questioned, feeling the suspension dip slightly as Freya slid into the passenger's seat of his car. She lowered the window, allowing the breeze to refresh the stale air. Her eyes never left the forest before her, as if she could still somehow see the tree house situated just ten minutes from this disused track.

"Yes," she confirmed, after a glance at her device where Alec's tracking information was displayed on screen.

"Then let's get her back home. She needs to understand her place," he growled. He glanced down as his device chimed a notification. The grip of his free hand tightened on the wheel until it creaked in protest. "We need to do this now."

The heat of the day had long receded, flooding the forest with mist as the cooler air brought from the cloudless skies descended. It was a beautiful woodland, filled with vibrant wildflowers and thriving trees. It was exactly how he remembered it as a child, a magical grove, a place straight from the pages of a fairytale.

The mist left a sweet taste of honeysuckle on their tongues as they walked to a place he knew all too well. The old tree house. It was no longer the glorious structure it had once been, and while time had been kind for leaving it standing, it had certainly worn it down, as it did with most things. Himself included.

He placed his hand to the hidden carving on the old tree trunk before casting his gaze above. The wooden floor failed to mask the sounds of pacing. The location was hidden, but one had to be silent to become obscure. With a nod, his escorts took their positions.

The climbing knots seemed too small for his hands now, far smaller than they had over twenty years ago. That Jesse had fled here seemed somehow ironic, he needed to know how that familiar had known of this location. Its existence had been a secret shared by few.

Jesse paced back and forth, a shroud of uneasiness settled firmly upon her shoulders. Levi, agitated by her distress, had taken to sitting on one of the boughs, maybe so he could alert her with an unpleasant growl when Alec finally returned. She was certain he only sat out there so his snarl could echo through the air and calm her when he came into view.

She had tried to sleep, but the nightmares kept her awake. She kept hearing Alec shouting for her, screaming her name, making her startle awake, but only the chorus of night creatures could be heard serenading the air. She had decided to give him one more hour, one more hour, and she and Levi would search for him themselves.

She tried to distract herself, first by running a comb through her tangled, dusty hair, then by arranging and rearranging the remaining splinters of wood from the table and chairs into vertical, then horizontal stacks, but nothing worked.

Removing a bottle of water from the pack, she had a sip. She'd deliberately not drunk much in case Alec came back when she had to relieve herself and assumed she was missing. But it was getting very late now, and she was more worried about whether he would return than when.

Taking a deep breath, she tried to relish the chorus of frogs and crickets outside as the night world came to life in song to serenade any who took the time to listen. She thought back to the days in her old bedroom, where she had sat pressed up against the bricked-in window, peering through the tiny central gap, listening for this song as she waited for the stars to shine.

Jesse's steps froze as she heard the shuffle of movement outside and a relieved smile spread across her face. She spun towards the door and put her free hand on her hip, trying to look stern, ready to wave her water bottle at him menacingly. Pursing her lips, she attempted to keep her expression firm, but could already feel the smile tugging at the corner of her mouth as the makeshift curtain parted.

"Alec where—" The water bottle slipped through her fingers, creating clean rivulets in the dirt encrusted floor as it exploded in mini waves at her feet. Her hands cupped her mouth as she backed away from Micah's hulking figure as he emerged from outside, looking furious.

As her vision strayed towards the small scar across his temple from the last time their paths had crossed, the glare upon his hardened face deepened, stealing the breath from her lungs. Her feet continued to slide backward, her gaze fixed to him while still searching for a means of escape. He looked angry, enraged, and all of it was focused firmly towards her. She felt the stone of the hearth press against her back and barely bit back a whimper.

"You're coming home," he growled, his deep voice reverberating in her ears and causing her skin to prickle with a cold sweat. Reaching back, she fumbled for the handle from the cast-iron pot, swinging it with all her strength as he advanced.

She knew she was trapped. In such close quarters there was no way would she make it to the door, let alone down the tree before he could grab her. She had to fight.

His forearm took the blow, his block reminding her of how Alec had moved, smooth, disciplined, trained. Before she knew what was happening, he had used the momentum from her overextended swing to duck behind her, his thick arms circling her waist as he dragged her backwards. Her fingers clawed on to the door frame, tearing the blanket from its precarious hanging as she attempted to gain purchase on something, anything, to stop him dragging her away. He snatched her towards him, forcing her grip to slip as he yanked her kicking and screaming towards the small hatch.

The hatch! Hope rekindled amid her desperate struggle, a struggle that Micah seemed to barely even notice. There was no way he could make the climb, not with her fighting him every step, she'd send them both plummeting from the footholds. Even though they'd both survive such a fall, it would present her a chance. All she needed to do was recover quicker, run quicker.

She felt him heaving her along as her heels dug into the platform, creating minor resistance until he kicked them from beneath her. She screamed, in surprise at first, until her stomach rose to her throat and the screams morphed into petrified silence as she felt herself thrown from the edge of the platform. She reached out, trying to grasp at branches, but the hurtling descent was clear of obstructions.

Her breathing froze as she plummeted hopelessly from the tree. She tried to twist in midair. If she could land with some grace, she could run through the pain, flee while he climbed down. She braced for impact, but instead of earth something soft cushioned her fall. The frameless life-net was wrapped around her flailing limbs before she'd even realised what had happened.

"Sedate her," Micah's growling voice commanded from above, drowning out all other sounds, even that of her pounding heart. She swallowed hard, seeing his monstrous silhouette looking down from the platform above and, for but a moment, she resigned herself to her fate. For but a moment, until she thought about Alec.

He had always been her safe place, a shelter in her mind that had become reality once he had returned. She was not going to lose him now, she would not give in, no one but him would ever touch her again. She had been cleansed by his love, her corruption burnt away by the fire of his passion. She would not be sullied again.

She kicked and screamed but instead of making progress her body just writhed as she remained trapped, wrapped like a corpse in a carpet, she thought soberly. The two people left holding her seemed to tighten their grasp while once slumbering birds took flight as the sound of her cries intensified. The sharp scratch that pierced her neck had almost gone unnoticed until she felt her limbs growing weaker and in the space of a slow, long blink Micah was towering over her. "I'd prefer for you to be coherent, but that can wait. Get her to the car."

She felt the rocking motion of movement before her world succumbed to darkness.

CHAPTER 8

Micah had parked his car on the old track that, many years ago, had once cut a path straight through to the old Birch estate. But like everything else belonging to that line, it had been left to decay. Until today he hadn't even stepped foot upon this land for over twenty years, but aside from the track being consumed by nature, and the shrubs and trees thriving, the area hadn't changed at all. It had always been rich with nature's glory.

Crickets sang in a dangerous chorus while the frogs ventured from the nearby river in search of food lured by their song. He closed his eyes, for a moment forgetting the fact he had a heavily sedated young woman being buckled into his car. He reached out, grasping Freya's hand as she stepped away from clipping Jesse into the middle seat.

"All secure, chief," Freya whispered, squeezing his hand lightly as she moved to stand beside him. "Whatever did you do to the lass? She's terrified of you."

"I cast a daunting figure." He shrugged. "Come, let's get her home."

Micah slid into the driver's seat, his vision flickering to the sleeping figure on his back seat. Her face was smeared with dirt, her newly coloured hair adorned by dried leaves, yet she looked every bit as lovely now as when he had seen her in her wedding gown. Perhaps more so, since her face was no longer twisted in anguish.

In this light, she was the image of her mother. His grasp tightened on the wheel as they pulled on to the main road. He had bought her from Lord Kyron and now she was about to discover what it meant to be—

Micah's ears rang. He shook his head, trying to clear the fog. It took a few moments for him to realise what had happened, to notice the rush of air coming from his shattered window. His limbs felt unresponsive as he raised his hand to his broken nose, his fingers slick with blood.

His movements felt slow and sluggish as he turned his head, his hand reaching out to Freya. He grasped her shoulder, pulling her back from the only deployed airbag. Its release had filled the car with the dust and smoke he hoped was responsible for the rattle sounding in his chest. Blood trickled down the side of Freya's face, perhaps from where the windscreen had exploded inward. She was breathing. Thank the gods, she was breathing.

His shoulders seized as he twisted again, fumbling to find the release for his belt. He blinked, hoping to clear his triple vision. Sound began to return. His engine spluttered pathetically, sounding muted against the tinnitus but, despite its shudders and coughs, it somehow kept running.

His head drooped for a second. He was so tired. It took more effort than he liked to force his eyelids open. The sound of two shots rang through the air, followed by the telltale sound of a seatbelt being released. He grasped again for his buckle release, but his arms were unresponsive, no longer even lifting at his demand.

"What about the others?"

"Medics are here. Leave them, let's hustle before we're IDed." Blue lights swarmed before his vision, highlighting the air before him until everything faded into darkness.

Jesse knew where she was before she had even dared to open her eyes. The blend of lavender and beeswax always stole her breath with its overpowering odour. There were times this scent had been so strong it had made her wheeze. What she didn't know, however, was why Micah had brought her here, of all places. Perhaps he had decided to sell her back after all, perhaps a quick lay wasn't worth the trouble she brought.

There was no doubt as to where she was, although part of her hoped, as she finally risked a peep through her heavy lashes, that she was wrong, that it was possible for two places to share the exact cloying odour of the room she had spent many years trying to escape. But the discomfort of the bedsprings where her weight pressed against the threadbare mattress had already warned her of the truth. She had no reason to hope. She knew exactly where she was.

As her unfocused vision began to clear, she almost succeeded in suppressing a groan. The springs on the worn-out mattress screeched under even her slightest movement, painfully digging into her through the virtually unpadded upholstery.

The figure staring back at her from the mirrored ceiling looked different, and it was a full few seconds before she remembered Alec rinsing the toner from her hair. She didn't like the colour. It had been a disguise, but now it just brought emphasis to her ghost-white pallor.

The bed screeched again as she moved, a sound that sent shivers chasing through her as images of fending off sweat-soaked attackers surfaced. The sound of her bed had become a chorus of shame. There was no sanctuary here.

She had almost been free and to hear it now brought back the feelings of shame and disgust, memories of Burnell's hand pressed against her mouth to muffle her cries, the way he forced her to look him in the eyes as he repeatedly defiled her. Eventually she learnt he didn't notice if her gaze strayed to the shatterproof mirrors he'd had installed, but to see the things he was doing to her was far worse than the lustful gleam in his eyes as he grunted above her.

"No," she whispered. She would not do this, she would not give her father any more power. He would never break her. No matter how many times she withstood his lash, nor how many times Burnell called upon her. Her will was made of steel, or to be precise, made from wood, mingled with the spicy scent of ginger and cinnamon, a place recently fortified by the new memories she had made.

Alec had come for her once, he would come for her again. Until then, she would endure whatever her father subjected her to.

Just as she had a place her mind would retreat, a safe place where Alec waited, so too did she have a vault where all her worst memories were stored along with the rawness of pain. No matter what they did, no matter how she suffered, she had always found solace in Alec's embrace. His presence kept her protected as she barricaded herself within the cottage in her mind. He was the reason her father had never broken her, the reason she felt strong. Oh, but to know those moments of freedom, once more to feel the grass and touch the trees, to remember so vividly all the things her father had stripped away by locking her here within this room.

In itself, being returned here was torture. She had known freedom, spent time with Alec clutched in her arms. It was sweet torture to have known such things, now lost. Her stomach clenched, wondering what could have happened to him, why he hadn't returned as he had promised.

For more years than she cared to remember, the window of this room was nothing more than a balistraria. Her original seat window had been bricked in and sealed, apart from a narrow slit, after she had once thrown herself through in the hope of an escape.

"It's about time you were waking up." Her father's voice startled her. He had been watching, an amused smirk upon his lips that caused his high cheekbones to rise and his blue eyes to sink. "So, pet, looks like you've been holding out on Daddy."

"I-I don't know what you mean," she whispered, sliding from the bed, backing into the corner of the room. She saw the flogger in his hand, heard the creak of the waxed leather as he flexed it, making her shiver. His eyes danced with mirth as he saw her gaze fix upon it. He chuckled as he slashed it through the air, its sound alone causing her back to burn instinctively in response to its all-too-familiar whoosh, knowing that sound was but a prelude of what was to come.

He approached slowly. The low heel of his boot—designed to add a few subtle inches to his height—made his footfall heavier. She tried to stand in defiance, to level her gaze upon him, yet as the neck of the flogger caressed her cheek, she flinched. She had a place to run, a place to push the pain, but that didn't mean she had no fear, that she didn't still endure each strike, she simply had a method of coping with what he did.

"Why not make this easier on us both? Bind your will to mine, use your gift for me and I will grant you your freedom." He pushed her chin upwards, his eyes shimmering. He recognised her defiance and liked what he was seeing. He was never one to do things the easy way, and she had never been one to give in without a fight.

"Never." He actually smiled. She saw it, his lips turning upwards in a smug satisfaction that stole her breath. It wasn't his normal smile, the one he wore when he had taught her a lesson. There was something more to it, something she couldn't read. He'd wanted her to refuse.

"Then you leave me no choice but to break and bind you by force."

"We both know you're not strong enough, or did the last fourteen years show you nothing of my resolve," she challenged, feeling brave. An ironic smile played upon her lips that made her look anything but pleasant.

"Oh, but I have a new weapon in my arsenal. But first, Burnell has being asking about you. He wants to play one more time before you're too broken to care." Her face dropped as she saw him standing in the doorway. His rotund figure was not quite balanced out by his height and breadth. The man was built like an American football player who had once been a wall of brawn, but now had long passed his prime. His once hard walls of muscle had been covered by his life of decadence and over indulgence. "Welcome home, pet." Her father's chuckle as he walked away, and the way he glanced over his shoulder as he pulled the door closed behind him, sent shivers through her core.

"What, no hug?" goaded Burnell, his face twisting into the sick grin she knew all too well. Her eyes grew wide. She had been free, she had escaped. Now she was here again, trapped, helpless. Her back remained pressed to the wall. She glanced around the room but knew better than to hope for anything to defend herself with.

It had been years since there had been any furniture in here. It had been removed the first time she had tried to barricade the door. The small room was bare, all but for her bed and the awful heavy-duty wardrobe she would sometimes spend days locked inside. She could see the padlock was fastened from where she stood, and for a moment was grateful for small mercies. "Don't play coy, you know what I want." His scent clung to her like acid, burning her skin. She wanted to run, but to where? The room was small. Once a walk-in wardrobe, this room had been converted to be her prison, a place where the chase of cat and mouse was put to an end, a place that left her nowhere to run.

Her legs betrayed her, freezing her in position. What the hell was she doing? She didn't freeze; she fought. She cried out as he grasped her hair, pulling her head back as he forced her to her knees. "Open wide, and if I feel even the slightest scrape of teeth, well, you remember what happened last time." Tears streamed down her face. She did remember. That had been the day she had finally given up hope, the day she stopped writing to Alec. She felt his hand grasp the collar, pulling her closer, harder, as he groaned, his other hand still tangled in her hair, controlling her every movement. "We should have collared you sooner." He mocked as she heaved, which only encouraged him further. "Come on, baby, show me how much you missed me."

"Enough." Her heart actually leapt when she heard his voice. Burnell's hand tightened in her hair for just a moment before he thrust her away to the floor. She looked up to Alec, her prince, the knight in shining armour who stood just outside her door. But something was wrong. His expression was unfamiliar, cold, and the way Burnell's lips twisted into a sneer caused her tears—the tears she had avoided shedding in his presence for years before her taste of freedom —to flow even quicker.

"I told you you'd enjoy this." He grinned, slapping Alec on his shoulder before zipping his trousers as he left. She looked up to him again. Something was wrong. This wasn't the boy she knew, the man she loved.

"What's wrong? You remember Alec, don't you?" her father asked from the doorway. "He works for me, after all. I thought for sure you would remember him, pet, especially since he's spent so many days in your bed."

In that moment, it was as if her world collapsed. Alec stepped inside the room. Gone were his casual clothes, replaced by a smart suit bearing the family crest, her family's crest. His expression remained cold and stony as he moved to stand beside her father, his hands behind his back, his feet shoulder width apart, just like a soldier. "The ritual is tonight. She need only be conscious." For one moment, as her father handed him the flogger, she swore she saw a flicker of emotion behind his eyes but it was gone too soon for her to even be sure it had been there.

"Alec, please," she whispered, searching his face for something familiar, some kind of recognition.

"Are you really that stupid, did you really not know? I saw you fleeing from Alvar's land, I knew you'd have to wait for the morning train, that's why I sent Alec to meet you. Don't tell me you thought it was fate, destiny? Your destiny is written by me." Her father was enjoying this too much, enjoying the sheer heartbreak that made pulling in a single breath feel impossible. The world around her blurred as all air seemed to be sucked from the room. Her father's smug expression told her all she needed to know. He knew he'd already won.

"Alec, tell me it's not true, please, tell me what we have means something to you." But his gaze remained fixed, his lips pressed tightly into a thin line. He said nothing, and the silence shattered her heart.

"Of course it's true. He works for me."

"Alec," she whispered, forcing the word through her grief-swollen throat.

"Alec has been training for my service for years. He knows how to break a person so completely they won't even remember their own name. As much as I would like to stay and watch him chip away at that iron will you have taunted me with for years, I have a ritual to prepare." She heard him chuckle as Alec locked the door behind him.

"Alec?" She searched his gaze for something, anything, the easy smile, a hint of regret for what she knew he was about to do. But his face was stoic, the mask of a soldier completely detached from the atrocity he was about to commit.

It had all been a lie, a manipulation so her father could finally get what he had wanted. The man she saw before, the one who held her in his arms and made her feel like a goddess, who had looked upon her with adoration, was gone. Nothing more than a childish dream, a deception.

None of it had been real, not one second, not one smile or kiss. Everything had been planned. Her father had known she would run, known there was but one way for her to leave. Everything was fake, schemed, and like a fool she had let herself believe it, let herself become vulnerable, show weakness. "Was everything between us just a game?"

Then she felt it, an excruciating pain that eclipsed everything she had endured before. The sting of the leather against her skin brought more than a welt to her flesh. She felt her soul cry, her heart shatter beyond repair.

She tried to push away the pain, to retreat into her safe place, but he was there too, the one person who had been her constant source of strength, her will when she was weak, was now the one who brandished the whip and sought to destroy her. His lies, his betrayal, had stripped everything from her, ensuring she felt every bite of the leather in both body and soul. "Please, Alec, don't." She hated the weakness in her voice, his impassive expression as the pain reduced her to her knees.

It was a lie.

Everything was a lie, and the force of this realisation hurt beyond the agony of each strike.

Alec's hands shook as he locked the door behind him, leaving her wounded, barely conscious just as he had been ordered to do. His feet carried him away, stilling the words he had wanted to scream. His eyes were dry, forbidden from showing remorse, forbidden from showing the regret that burned his soul.

Internally, he had screamed and cried, fought with every ounce of strength he had. But it had not been enough. He cursed his hand as it brought the whip down on her time and time again. The look in her eyes had been his destruction, she'd believed every word her father had said. She thought everything they had shared was just part of his plan to destroy her. And he had certainly done that. He had seen it all too clearly.

Each blink of his eyes brought back another image of her crying out, of his hands, the hands that should have protected her, causing her pain. As the door to his room closed, the command released and the tears finally appeared.

'Do not speak. Show her no remorse, show no love, break her will completely, take her to the brink of unconsciousness. Do whatever it takes to break her.' His master's command echoed around his mind. He had fought it, how he had fought. If ever there was a chance, a command he could resist, it should have been this one. All of his arro-

gant thoughts about his will, about being strong enough to rebel, had come to nought.

He was weak.

He had been powerless to disobey. His heart ached. The heel of his hand beat against his chest as his heart threatened to tear itself in two. *Traitor, traitor, traitor,* it beat. He would never forget seeing the moment her heart shattered. Twice he had witnessed her destruction in her eyes, the first time when he'd taken the whip from her father, and again as she finally broke by his hand and she lost the will to fight.

Because of him, she would be bound to Lord Kyron, just as he was. Because of him, she would know no freedom, no happiness, and happiness was *all* she deserved, but he had taken every grain, every hope from her. He had seen her die inside, her strength and will extinguished, all by his own traitorous hand.

He remembered the sound of every blow, her every scream and tear that pierced his soul like daggers of ice. He wanted to shout out, to explain he was not acting of his own will. That he loved her, that he was sorry. But the words wouldn't come, the words would never come. When she asked if it had all been a game, he wanted nothing more than to take her in his arms and whisper comfort, yet instead he brought the whip down. Time and time again.

"Damn it," he whispered. Each of her sobs had cut through him, creating invisible scars to match the ones she would bear by his hand. "Damn it." His voice broke as tears streamed down his face in endless supply. "Damn it." His fist struck the wall, each strike accompanied by a despairing expletive.

He had wanted to protect her, to shelter her from this, not be the one responsible. His hands were raw, knuckles bleeding. He wished he could feel numb, but knew he deserved every moment of this anguish and more. "Damn it." He sank to his knees in sobs, staring disdainfully at his hands, the hands that hurt the woman he loved and were now marred by his own blood as much as they were with hers. "Damn it," he whispered, praying his heart would make true its threat to stop. *Traitor, traitor, traitor.*

"Is she prepared?" He hated the smug sound of his master's voice as he let himself into his room. The sky had turned dark. At some point, day had become night and now was the time for all that was light to forever be extinguished. "A stab to the body heals, but a wound to the soul is eternal. It seems you both learnt an important lesson today. Let's hope it is not one I need have you repeat."

CHAPTER 9

As Burnell escorted her down the hallway, Jesse could not even muster the energy to feel repulsed by his touch. What was the point? Fighting never got her anywhere, anyway.

Never before had she felt so hollow, so empty. Her shoulder collided with the wall, leaving a streak of semi-dried blood along the wallpaper. Her every muscle, her every wound screamed, yet they were nothing. The pain of her body was nothing compared to that of her heart and soul. It was difficult to breathe, each breath, each beat of her heart brought fresh agony. How she wished it would end.

As she exhaled, she held her breath, but the pain didn't stop. Her heart didn't stop, despite how much she wished to be free of the pain.

"Keep movin'." Burnell shoved her. She hadn't even realised she'd stopped walking. Her knees felt like rubber, buckling weakly every few steps. She had trusted Alec, thought they had something special. He hadn't even needed to strike her, his betrayal had been her undoing, and it had all started with that kiss. Nothing mattered any more. She had fought for years, never giving up, no matter how tired she was, how much pain she endured. But she was done. The one thing she had held on to had been a lie.

Burnell's hand thrust between her shoulders, sending her skidding across the rough stone floor towards their family altar. Then he turned and left. She lay there weakly and closed her eyes. This was the first time she had set foot inside this room. Although she had peered within a few times as a child, she never had the courage to enter, nor understood why they had needed such a place.

The entire room was as grey as a stormy day. Scant light flickered from wall-mounted sconces, casting dim reflections on the highly polished lead tablets nailed to the wall at the far end of the room. Meanwhile, the small hearth burnt fiercely, adding a sickening heat to the air. She had always thought the tablets' presence behind the small marble altar to be strange, but she had never dared to step beyond the door.

Her father stood behind the altar now, watching her with sinister delight. She cursed her heart, because, as she saw Alec standing in the far corner of the room, it had still leapt. Treacherous heart. How could it still beat for him? She lowered her head back to the stone floor, feeling its grainy texture against her cheek she closed her eyes, but they wouldn't stay shut, they gravitated towards him. Curse her heart. It loved him still. He had betrayed her, and now so too did her heart, because it told her with each and every beat that it would only ever belong to him.

Alec, the stranger, a man nothing more than a shadow of a memory, stood silently. Watching with indifference as her father placed a lead tablet upon the altar stone. A katadesmos, she knew what they were now. Given what her father intended to do it was the only thing powerful enough for him to complete the rite.

"On your knees," he ordered. She heard him, even considered obeying, but her body would no longer move. For the first time, she wondered where Levi was. He had been with her when Micah had entered the tree house, yet he hadn't thought to warn her of the danger. Had this spirit betrayed her, too? Her dry eyes burned. At least she couldn't cry. Her father wouldn't get the satisfaction of another tear. They had been destroyed, along with her heart and soul.

When she didn't move, he nodded to Alec, who wordlessly approached. The touch of his hands on her fresh wounds burnt as he manhandled her, dragging her to her knees where she sat with shoulders slumped, awaiting the end. If she was lucky, what he would do to her would strip her of this pain.

With another nod, her father dismissed Alec back to his place. Now her father stood before her, his twisted smile casting demonic shadows on his face as he leaned towards her. His hands grasped the back of the collar. She was barely aware of the sound of it releasing. Or of what it meant.

Her vision shifted, her world changing to perceive the aura of magic becoming more beautiful and vibrant, yet to her the world was simply black and grey now, nothing but darkness and shadow, empty and hollow.

Her father's bear essence stood beside him at the altar on hind legs. The glowing of the two adjoining auras suggested he was drawing power from both parts of his soul. The crackle of embers returned her attention to the hearth, and for the first time she noticed the glowing branding iron. Another scar, she wondered if she'd even feel it when her soul was already in such agony she didn't understand how she still lived.

The tug in her mind was subtle at first, a little like when Levi beckoned for her attention. Dark tendrils extended from her father's aura towards her, wrapping her in its dark stifling embrace as she became aware of his presence invading her mind.

For the briefest moment, by instinct alone, she resisted. Sought the safe place within her mind. But her cottage lay in ruins, the once vibrant garden had withered and died. Her cottage burned, ash spiralling into the night sky to eclipse the stars. Upon its ruined embers stood Alec. His back was to her, but she knew it wasn't her Alec, the Alec who had sheltered her here for years. He turned slowly. His gaze pierced her as he stood upon the burning embers, watching her with a dark smile as he clutched the flogger within his hand.

She gasped, pulling her mind away. He had truly taken everything. Her father's pressure within her core confirmed he was succeeding, she could feel herself slipping away. But she had already lost her soul. What did it matter now if her father claimed its tattered remains?

∽

Micah groaned, the feeling of a hand in his own was a momentary reprieve before a burning pain enveloped his torso. He heard himself gasp as he pushed himself up, the uncomfortable tightness of his side bringing his focus to the dressings wrapped tightly around his stomach.

What the hell had happened? He remembered a crash, gunshots, Jesse! He sucked in a breath, ripping the drip from his arm, sending a spray of crimson fluid across the sterile white floor. He sat up too quickly, tearing the wires from his chest to cause the nearby machine to blare in alarm before he saw Freya was standing before him, her hands on his shoulders. He wasn't sure how she had navigated around the far-too-small bed so quickly without his notice. She looked tired, dark circles ringing her tear-filled eyes. Why had she been crying?

"Freya?" he rasped.

"Lie back down, you big lug," she choked out through tears. The pale strips of the butterfly stitches on her forehead seemed to glow against her dark skin, drawing his focus to her injury, away from her tears.

"What happened? I thought we were in a crash." Dismissing her request, he felt a sweat break out on his brow as he pushed himself to stand, ignoring the wave of nausea that accompanied the dark motes swimming across his vision. He needed to get out of here.

"We were. They took Jesse and shot you." He searched his memories and remembered hearing shots from the back before blacking out. He hadn't even felt them. His stomach burned again.

"How long? How long have I being lying here uselessly?" His bare feet shuffled across the cold floor. His arm clasped his side as he struggled to breathe. It shouldn't hurt this much, he should heal faster.

"They had to operate. You were in surgery for six hours—"

"How long?" he growled. Surgery, well, that explained the pain at least, but he shouldn't have needed to go under the knife. Most doctors simply forced the shifter side to emerge through ethereal stimulation, and the act of shifting allowed accelerated healing. Something had to have stopped the transformation, it was the only explanation.

"About fifteen hours."

"Then there's still time." His knees buckled. Why was he feeling so weak? Freya grasped him as his hand reached out for the cluttered bedside table. It moved slightly on the wheels, causing him to twist in an attempt to keep his balance. Pain turned his vision black and suddenly he was on his knees. Sweat dripped from his jaw, counting away the wasted seconds in a soft patter as his gaze refocused on the floor, watching another drop of sweat explode on the tiles to mingle with the blood from when he had torn out the needle. It pained him how few steps he had taken.

"You lost a lot of blood. The bullets were coated with some form of toxin that stopped you shifting." Freya crouched before him, her concern clearly evident in her dark eyes.

"Figured as much." He crawled forward on his hands and knees until he reached the chair and fought his way to his feet. He winced. Snatching his folded jacket from the chair, he wrapped it over the gown before struggling into his trousers.

"You're not serious? You need to rest," Freya scolded, her hands on her hips making her look like a force he normally wouldn't dare to argue with.

"Later," he growled, trying to shrug her away as she grasped his arm. "No time."

"What do you mean?"

"Where. Is. Jesse?" Heat washed over him as he staggered towards the door, barely making it to the small porcelain basin before bile and acid poured from his mouth in sour heaves. He retched again, his stomach aflame. He hoped the basin had been well secured, because he knew at the moment it was the only thing standing between himself and the floor.

"She's not here."

"And you didn't think to send anyone to look for her?"

"Mister Alvar, you shouldn't be out of bed." A hand grasped his arm gently. It wasn't Freya's. Panting labouredly, he glanced around seeing his room was filled with apprehensive-looking nurses and medics, but he had no idea when they had arrived.

"Unhand me woman," he snarled, causing the Blue Coat he had just seen stationed at the door to glance over his shoulder. "You, Blue Coat." He clicked his fingers. The young man seemed to turn too slowly. "I'm invoking Clan Animus. One of my clan has been abducted." Clan Animus was a rarely invoked aspect of the law where a clan alpha could intervene if one of his clan members had been wronged. It was usually invoked in cases such as these where someone was believed to be in immediate danger unless action was taken.

It allowed him to be present to ensure his clan's protection and bear witness to events. Being a clan matter, he could have legally handled it within the confines of the law, but initiating this right meant the Blue Coats were obligated to help him and, at the moment, he needed all the help he could get. The drawback was, he had to be there to claim her physically. He took three staggering paces, the cool smell of the fresh air coming from somewhere beyond the door revitalising him, driving him onward.

"Micah." Freya's hand replaced the nurse's. "We don't know that..."

"Don't you check my messages? Kyron plans to turn Jesse into his familiar. If we don't claim her back, it will be too late. It may already be too late." His arm pressed against his stomach as he bit back a groan, while his other slid across the wall, guiding his slow retreat.

"Sir, are you certain about invoking Clan Animus?"

"He has Jesse, his own fucking man told me." He twisted, wresting his device from his pocket and presenting it to the Blue Coat, who studied it intently, a frown creasing his features as his arm slipped under Micah's shoulder, supporting his burly weight, using the motion to slip Micah's device back into his pocket.

"Can you tell me exactly what happened? Who are we retrieving?" The officer questioned, his fingers already typing an alert. Micah only hoped it was one in his favour and not some manner of section document. He could not afford to be held here. Time was running out.

"Jesse Kyron."

"Our lord's daughter? Are you..."

"Freya, send the..." He glanced at the emblem on the Blue Coat's sleeve. "Send the Leftenant the transfer of clan agreement." Freya did as instructed. He took a second, while still supporting Micah's enormous form, to look at the documentation, a crease wrinkling his otherwise youthful brow.

"You purchased her? That's highly irregular."

"She's my clan and is currently being held contrary to my wishes. It is not the first time he has attempted to retrieve her," Micah snarled, taking another slow, lurching step forward.

"Are you saying he is responsible for the attempt on your life?"

"You think that's what this was?" Micah grimaced. "No, this was all about her, and he's got enough contacts that I can't prove anything. What I can prove is she's with him now, and in danger."

"Surely you can't really think he'd do anything untoward? She's his daughter. Are you certain you can trust your source?"

"Nothing untoward? She has more scars than any soldier I have fought beside, and they're just the visible ones. He's abducted a member of my clan. It cannot be left unaddressed. Take me there now under Clan Animus."

"Very well. We will escort you to Lord Kyron and you can answer my questions en route." An awaiting orderly approached as the Leftenant nodded. Micah sighed in relief as he lowered himself into the wheelchair. Time was too short for him to be proud.

Micah stood propped against the door, his face twisted in a combination of pain and annoyance. The Blue Coats, under Clan Animus, had full access to the property, but Micah hadn't needed them to complete a full search. He knew exactly where she was. The Leftenant had helped him stagger there. The distance from the rear doors to the small altar room, overlooked by the rear staircase, had seemed so much further than the short distance he had hobbled.

As the door opened and he saw her on her knees, without the fire or moxie he had seen her display, he feared they were already too late. Her white T-shirt was torn, red and pink stains altering the once pure colour. She knelt, staring vacantly towards the floor while her father chanted.

"Everybody remain still." Lord Kyron's incantation stopped the second he heard the Leftenant's demand and a flash of annoyance passed over his chiselled face, only to be quickly erased with a well-practised smile.

Jesse, as if suddenly released from some unseen tension, folded sideways, her eyes still open as she lay paralysed, unmoving, simply staring ahead in the same blank manner. The hand Micah was not using to support his weight balled into a tight fist. "I am here to claim Jesse Kyron. She is my clan and you are holding her against my wishes." Micah's voice came out hoarse, causing him to cough. As he clutched his stomach, he saw the amusement flicker in Lord Kyron's eyes. He looked down on them from his position at the altar, his hands resting gently on the smooth surface.

"Now, now, there must be a misunderstanding. My daughter came to me wanting this. She said you consented." Honey dripped from his tone, appeasing to the ears of the Blue Coats who listened. Micah knew at once that no one would challenge the word of this town's lord, not without clear evidence. "If you're saying you had no awareness, by all means retrieve what is yours. I would hate to create a rift between our clans."

"A misunderstanding? Are those marks across her flesh a misunderstanding, too?" he growled, his gaze once more falling to Jesse's blood-stained garments.

"I was concerned too, naturally. I just assumed they happened during the accident she said she was in on her way home to me." Micah growled again at his words.

"Is the matter settled?" asked the Leftenant dubiously. There was something in the weight of his stare, a desperation that asked Micah to provide evidence that proved Lord Kyron's words to be false. His hand still rested on his weapon, another clear sign he was one of the few officers in this town's law enforcement not in the pockets of the lord.

The problem was, there was no evidence, not unless Jesse herself was willing to talk and, in her current condition, the fact her eyes were even open was a testament to her strength. Even if she did level an accusation, it would become his word against hers, and he was bound to have an airtight reason he was not involved in whatever charges were brought against him.

"I have a plethora of people who will testify she came to me willingly and in this condition." He cast his gaze towards Alec, then smugly to the plaques on the wall behind him. His meaning was clear. "If she wasn't of sound mind, and remembers things incorrectly, I have many people who witnessed her return." His lips curled as his gaze met Micah's. He knew he had won.

"The matter is settled, for now. But she will not be entering your service. This is my final word on the matter as alpha of the Alvar clan." Micah stepped aside, nodding to Freya. He watched as the woman, previously kept outside of the room by a restraining grasp of a Blue Coat, hurried inside.

She took barely a moment to examine the young woman on the floor, before pulling her to her feet, supporting more than her share of the young woman's weight as she guided Jesse's shuffling and exhausted figure through the door. Micah turned to follow, hearing Lord Kyrons low, growled warning.

"You should keep an eye on that clan of yours. If you can't control it, I know someone who can."

CHAPTER 10

Freya had escorted Jesse to the same room she had escaped from just five days ago. It was one of the larger rooms in the manor, and had been dubbed the timbre suite, since most of the furnishing, including the panelled walls, had been made from high-quality wood. It was also one of the few rooms to have its own en-suite bathroom, which in the case of this room, had been hidden behind the panelling to give it a secret passage kind of feel. In preparation for her return, the room had been emptied of all furnishings but for the large, heavy four-poster bed which sat on a thick woven rug to stop the polished wooden floor being scuffed.

Jesse didn't even tense as she was escorted inside. Freya watched her reactions from the corner of her eyes, her resigned posture showing some signs of awareness from the otherwise disengaged woman. Despite Freya's best attempts, she hadn't coaxed a single word from her. She had even needed to support her hand to lift a bottle of water to her lips when they had reached the Blue Coat's vehicle that brought them home.

When Freya excused herself to fetch medical supplies in preparation for cleaning Jesse's wounds, she had thought she may have relaxed, but she hadn't even moved from where she had been sat on the edge of the bed, not a muscle.

Seeing the young woman, who had once had so much fight she felled a powerful alpha with a single blow, reduced to nothing more than a shell was heartbreaking. Not a single reaction had been teased from her, not as Freya carefully soaked the dried blood from her top until she could peel it away, nor as she treated the open wounds with antiseptic before carefully dressing them. Freya's heart ached for her. The scars this young woman bore told tales of a life no one should have had to endure.

She was just emerging from the bathroom after pouring away the pink-tinted fluid when Micah entered, earning her first reaction. It was subtle, something she may have missed if she hadn't been watching her so closely. Jesse's hands had tightened ever so slightly on the bedding beneath her.

"How bad?" he growled, following Freya with his eyes as she stepped from the bathroom, sealing the invisible panel door behind her with a firm push. For a few seconds she didn't have the words, so simply shook her head.

"The lass hasn't spoken a word. I'm not sure she's even with us." As she answered she grasped the long nightgown from the door handle, bunching it in her hands attempting to cover Jesse quickly to allow some semblance of dignity. Jesse's arm raised, weakly pushing the garment away.

"I won't fight," she whispered, her voice so small and deflated Freya had almost missed what she had said.

"Why would you need to fight?" Freya questioned.

"I don't need to be of sound mind to open my legs." She heard Micah growl a curse before he stormed from the room. The slamming of the door sent echoing vibrations throughout every wooden surface. Freya hooked the nightgown over Jesse's head before she had the chance to protest again, before she hurried after him.

Micah stood outside the door, his eyes molten with fury as they glared at the landscape picture on the wall, wishing the picturesque image would bring even a measure of serenity. Having now managed to shift, his wounds were already much better, his vision burned now for a different reason entirely. He tensed slightly as Freya slid from the bedroom, closing it softly behind her before she took him in her arms to plant a delicate kiss on his scarred brow.

"I never realised what that tyrant was putting her through. Adeline would turn in her grave if she saw those scars. We should have got to her sooner." His fist clenched, his only comfort coming from Freya's cool caress.

"Why would she think you wanted..." Her hands slid to his shoulder, so he had no choice but to look down and meet her gaze.

"She must have heard me speaking to her father. I swear, Freya, when I went in to her, I told her everything, but she was hysterical. I don't know how much of what I said even got through. I admit, maybe I was too heavy-handed, but she was feral, she just wouldn't listen." Micah let his head fall back against the wall. She should have realised the truth by now. She'd even taken his wallet, so she had to have seen the photograph. And yet, each time their paths had crossed, she had attacked him as if her very life depended on it.

"You've got to talk to her, let her know she's safe. She doesn't have a clue what's going on, and whatever they did to break her, really did. She's a strong lass. It would've taken more than just another thrashing to dim her soul, I mean just look at what she did to you." Freya traced her finger across the small scar on his temple. He smiled weakly. He'd admired her strength that day. There weren't many who could hold their own against him, even when taking him by surprise.

"Alec," he growled in understanding. "He used the fucking familiar." It had been obvious what he had done. The way Alec had just stood there unmoving as they entered the altar room, his hollow empty gaze watching, seeing all, but never showing any reaction. He hadn't moved because he'd been told to watch. Lord Kyron had used Alec to bend her to his will and, given her strength, he had probably been the only person who could, especially after they had spent so many days together renewing their bond.

Micah took a deep breath. He needed to salvage this situation, and soon, before she lost herself completely, before no spark of life remained. His anger bristled as, seeing him enter the room, she submissively lifted her legs on to the bed without even a thought to the rawness of her injuries.

"Cut that out," he growled impatiently as she began to raise the hem of the nightdress. Freya bustled past, snatching the hem down and pulling her back to her seated position. "The things you heard me say, I only said for his benefit. Jesse," Micah went on. "*Freya* is my wife and I would *never* touch another woman. Never."

"You never actually told her?" He knew what Freya was doing, steering the conversation, making sure the words had time to register. He'd just told her he'd explained everything to her, but she was trying to create a rapport between them. "You big lug, no wonder she's been running from you. Jesse, kitten, Micah doesn't want to hurt you. He's your uncle."

"My..." Her voice was so small, but there was something more than just resignation there. His niece was still in there. She was hurting, gods how she was hurting, but she had responded. She was reachable.

"Your uncle," he confirmed. "I'm Adeline's little brother. Didn't you see the picture of her in my wallet? I've been trying to get you away from your father for years. I petitioned the Blue Coats when your father killed her." He saw the look on her face, the stirring of the emotions once blanked, and he continued, hoping to drag just part of her from the void in which she had lost herself. "Yeah, I know what happened. I tried to get an investigation, but he had everyone in his pocket. Your mother was sold to him at seventeen. I was only seven at the time and didn't really understand what was going on, only that the young lord wanted to marry my sister.

"Our parents agreed to his request of purchase to strengthen the clan, to create an heir and an alliance, but it backfired. After the wedding your father arranged an accident, killing our parents and defaulting the estate to her as the only surviving heir.

"When you were born, he refused to allow you to be registered. By not giving you a chip, it meant those of your mother's clan couldn't have any claim to you, no matter the circumstances. But, just to be certain, he methodically eliminated anyone who refused to swear loyalty to a new alpha. Once the clan had been abolished, he knew no one could get their hands on you within the confines of the law, no matter what he did."

"My mother's maiden name was..."

"Birch," he interjected, moving to perch himself beside her on the bed. The mattress dipped slightly under his weight. "The accident that took my parents should have killed me too and, for my own safety, our clan let him think it had. I was adopted discreetly and my surname changed. I took Freya's name when we married. When she ascended to leader, we used her clan's status and resources to petition an allegiance through marriage. It was the only way we could get a legal right of access to you.

"The wedding was a sham. The officiant already knew what we had planned, which is why we took the contract without marriage being a stipulation. We purchased you from your father in exchange for money and influence that we had ensured he desperately needed.

"When I tracked you down after you ran and saw you with Alec, I knew I had to try to get you away from him as soon as I could. Even if your mother told me you were soul-bonded, he's still your father's familiar. It was only a matter of time before he led him back to you. That's why we grabbed you when we did." Micah rubbed his arm, recalling how she had struck him with the cast-iron pot from his own hideaway. The place where he and his sister would meet in secret whenever she could steal away.

"He's what?" There it was again, a stirring of emotion, raw, something other than the blank stare she had possessed since he'd retrieved her. He saw her muscle tense, her grip clenching the bedding at her fingertips as her breathing deepened. Rage. Micah could see her rage and it was burning through the void, consuming her every fibre.

"Didn't you know, kitten?" Freya crouched before her, placing a comforting hand on her knees, holding Jesse's gaze. Micah watched her with adoration. How he loved that woman, she had a way with people that he was lacking. "Alec's family have been serving yours for the past two hundred years. He was born a familiar, his will completely bound before his first septennial." More rage, more anger.

"How do you know this?" Her voice was stronger, something beyond a timid whisper.

"Your mother told me," Micah replied. Following Freya's lead, he placed his large hand on her shoulder, awkwardly patting it for a moment before drawing back. "She knew I hadn't died in the accident and arranged to meet me in our old tree house. She told me she was planning to destroy the katadesmos binding Alec. I think that was what she had been doing when he murdered her. She knew if your father discovered you were soul-bound he'd find a way to use your connection against you, and your power is one that could bring the shifter world to its knees."

"My power?"

"The Birch line has been adapting for generations, the females can see nature and essence spirits. But you, you completed the transition. You are the first who can physically interact with them, like you did with me the day you ran from this room. If your father were to get that power, he could hold the entire elder bloodlines hostage, those with other-selves, at least."

"It's bad enough your daddy has been using that boy of yours to drive part of the insurrection, but if he had your gift..." Freya shook her head. "I'm just glad we got to you when we did."

"How did you find me?" Rage now simmered beneath her every word. He could only imagine what she was thinking, but if this was the buffer she needed to draw herself back, then who was he to question it? She had endured more than he could imagine, and if this was how she had kept herself sane and strong, then so be it.

"Alec. I don't know how he managed to do it, but the lad sent a notification to our clan saying your father intended to bind you," Micah revealed. "But it wasn't just once, it was many times, and each was a small miracle. He should not have been able to do what he did. Telling us was clearly against his master's interests, and yet somehow he still succeeded."

"How?"

"Your daddy must not have ordered him not to. He's a clever boy, he loves you so much he found a way around his orders, the scintilla of a loophole."

"He loves me?" she spat venomously, her once-blank expression warping to incredulity as the first sign of tears welled in her eyes, and while they chilled his heart they also warmed it. Her fire was returning. "Did he love me when he took my father's flogger, when he did this to me, when he shattered everything I was while looking in my eyes without remorse, without regret?

"You have it wrong. My father sent him to find me, he let us have time together to remind me how much I'd loved him, all to make the betrayal cut deeper, to shatter my will to fight. And you know what?" she gasped between sobs, "he did. He didn't just strike my body, he shattered my soul and now there's nothing left, nothing worth salvaging.

"My father is welcome to it, I just don't care any more. The one thing, the one person who had kept me going all this time, the one person I trusted and thought would truly protect me, dealt the deepest blow, the most fatal, and it's not even one that can be seen." Angry tears streaked her face. Micah watched his wife wrap her arms gently around Jesse's shoulders, pulling her close. He blinked hard. So anger hadn't been her buffer all those years, it had been the thought of Alec.

Lord Kyron would pay for this.

"Alec did this to you?" Freya questioned softly, but he could hear the heartbreak in his wife's gentle tone. "Oh, kitten, he's a familiar. He wouldn't have had a choice. If your daddy ordered him, there's nothing that could stop him from obeying. Maybe if he'd not been bound by blood from birth, then the bond you two share might have made a difference, but he was born into servitude.

"But if there's one thing we know for certain, it's that he loves you. He didn't want to do this or he wouldn't have found a way to warn us. He doesn't even know we're allies, to him we're just the lesser evil, the only ones who could go in with a legal right to claim you.

"Can't you see, he didn't want you to end up like him? He knew what your daddy had planned and did the only thing he could to stop it. You can't possibly understand how unprecedented something like that is. How desperate he must have been. Something like that only comes from a place of love."

"It's true, Jesse. He sent me a notification when we were already on our way for you and, when I woke up in hospital, there were over twenty more begging us to come for you. He was desperate. It takes a strong will to find a loophole in a master's command, and it takes a stronger will even to attempt such a resistance.

"It's more than I've known any familiar achieve before. If your father wanted to use him to break you, his orders will have been clear and well defined to ensure you had no way of knowing. The fact he got notifications to me shows how desperate he was."

"How desperate he was? What about me? He betrayed me, and these welts and lacerations are nothing. He destroyed me, and he did so with a smile."

"Jesse, the lad loves you. Anything he did to you was because your father willed it to be so. He's a familiar, his master's word is law. A familiar just obeys, most of the time they don't even realise they are acting against their own choices, and I swear, I've never heard of one managing to circumvent their master's orders in even the most dire situations, not until today."

Jesse couldn't believe what she was hearing. Alec had been her father's familiar all along. How was that even possible, how could she not have known? Heated rage simmered within her, each heartbeat pumping acid through her veins. Her father had known of their connection. The more she listened to what Micah and Freya were saying the more she realised he had not only forced Alec to hurt her, but was probably responsible for the things Alec had mentioned in the letter she wasn't supposed to have seen, the mistakes and the things he wasn't proud of that he thought could never be forgiven. All this time, he had been as much of a prisoner as she had. Only his sentence had already stripped him of his choices.

Alec had been her father's familiar his entire life, bent to his will, forced into his service. It seemed her mother had thought he was her soulmate. She had given her life trying to free him because she had known exactly how her father would use him. She gave her life hoping to avoid this exact situation.

Rage could not come close to how she felt. It was something more, something primal, and it was her crutch, her strength. Her own father had corrupted her soulmate, turning him into a weapon to be wielded against her. At least now she understood the tether she had once seen between their hearts, a tether that had disappeared the moment he had struck her.

She had always been told soulmates were rare, perhaps even an old wives' tale, an ancient lore. Love, now that was something she had read about, had felt. But soulmates were an outdated principle, or so she had thought. But if fairy tales were true, if he had really been her soulmate, why hadn't he been able to fight the command? True love should conquer all, so why couldn't it overpower the bond of a familiar when he was being forced to hurt his other half? Part of her knew the answer, it was as she had been told, he was a familiar long before their paths had crossed, even if he hadn't sworn his oath, his blood was already a prison.

She pushed her hands through her hair, linking her fingers at the back of her neck as she took a deep breath. Freya and Micah were watching her intently, neither saying a word. Her skin burned, her soul was in agony, but as much as she wanted to hate him right now, as much as the thought of him caused her heart to tear, part of her still wanted to believe what they had shared was real.

Gods, she really was a fool.

After everything, she still wanted to hold on to just a fragment of him. But if what Micah said was true, if Alec was bound to her father, his will no longer his own, then—*but it had still been his hand*—she reminded herself, her thoughts streaming in a constant disorientating loop. She looked towards Levi who, for the first time, seemed to avoid her gaze. *No wonder Levi had growled at him, he'd known he would hurt me,* she thought. Maybe it had been unwillingly, but the image of him haunted her each and every time she blinked.

"Can I free him?" No, this wasn't right, despite what he had done she would not stand for this. Not if it was in her power to fix it. "If he belongs to the family, he belongs to me too, right?" Her own voice was barely a ghost of a whisper. What he did to her should be unforgivable, but to leave him subjected to her father's will, to leave him without a choice, was something she could not condone. He deserved his own life, he deserved a chance of freedom, as much as she had. Perhaps he could still be saved before her father crushed him too.

"It's not impossible. Your mother thought she'd found a way, but you'd need to form a connection with his shifter. A familiar bond executed via blood and katadesmos only binds the human essence. Only a witch can bind the animal. A witch or a druid. If you can force him to shift, then your father won't be able to command him.

"Given your skills, you should be able to interact with his human-self despite him being in animal form, and have his animal become yours, that way, even with your father's command vying for control you should be able to keep him shifted. Your father owns the man, you own the animal. It isn't a solution, but it means your father can't use him against you while we seek a permanent answer."

"Alec doesn't have a shifter essence." She had known Alec all her life. At the age of seven, when his shifter essence should have been strong enough to materialise, Alec's essence never split. He remained alone.

"Impossible, your mother said—"

"He doesn't," she snapped, cutting Micah off. "Never has. His aura lacks the shimmer and I've never seen him with another creature."

"Then the only chance we have is destroying the katadesmos. You have his blood in your veins, but since you aren't the Kyron clan's leader, there is no guarantee it will respond to you since the ties are linked to the family head," Micah advised.

"But, kitten, if we're going to do this you gotta be prepared for your daddy to use him against you again. But it won't be him, remember that. No matter what your daddy makes him do, know that he is fighting inside, as impossible as it seems. Just remember he can't control his actions, no matter how contrary they are to his own desires.

"Before you do anything like that though, kitten, you need to heal. Better if you shift to speed the process," Freya advised softly, her eyes filled with sympathy.

"I'm not a shifter. I can connect with other people's essences, it seems, but I don't have one of my own, just like Alec. I'm surprised you haven't heard rumours of the Kyron Clan curse."

"So who is that?" she asked, glancing towards Levi. Jesse frowned. No one had noticed him before, and it made her question why Freya could see him.

"That's Levi, he's been with me since I was a child. He was the first spirit I saw. Since I'm a druid, I guess he's some kind of spirit guardian. How can you see him?"

"I can't see him so much as sense him. We cat people can sense when other similar essences are near. Can you tap into him?" she asked.

"We aren't tethered."

"You weren't tethered to me, either, but that didn't stop you using my strength and shifter against me," Micah added.

"To be honest, I didn't realise I could do that. I just panicked." If she had known she was capable of such things, her life would have been much different.

"Then before anything else, kitten, get some rest. Tomorrow we'll see what you can do." Freya rose to her feet, tracing her hand down Jesse's arm. "We're just at the end of the hall if you need anything. Do you want any pain relief?"

"No." No she didn't. She wanted to feel each raw and excruciating sensation because the pain filled her with rage and right now she needed that. She needed her anger, because it was the only way she could bring herself to free Alec. No matter what he did, he didn't deserve the future that awaited him.

Once he was free, she could move on, leave this world behind without regret.

The pain in her chest intensified, and she knew to embrace it completely would be to slip away. But first, she would free him. One of them should live on. Once her rage died and she became empty once more, she could finally rest. After this one last thing, she was truly done.

She had endured more pain than any one person should. She had nothing left anymore, not even dreams, and she was ready to sleep. But before peace came vengeance, and for that she needed rage.

She glanced towards Micah and Freya as they left. She had never imagined they were family, that part of her mother still lived on, which is why she had no intention of revealing her true intentions. She would free Alec, but she would also ensure her father paid. She had nothing left to lose and if she was going, by the gods she would take him with her.

Rage was all she needed now.

CHAPTER 11

Jesse crept through the house on tiptoes. She had waited until Freya had looked in on her and the deep reverberation of Micah's voice had faded into quiet snores. The Alvar home was amazing, as would be expected for a clan alpha. It was grand without being grandiose or overbearing. The thick plush carpet of the staircase was soft beneath her feet, muffling any sound of her footfall, should anyone be listening. The kitchen, however, had been tiled, and each step padded upon the cool surface.

"I wasn't doing nothin'," a small voice said defensively. The freezer was open. Its light, along with the ring of chocolate around the young girl's mouth, betrayed the lie. Jesse's gaze strayed towards the back door, but the girl had already seen her. Her dark eyes, that looked overly large and deer-like from having been discovered, reminded her of Freya.

"I won't say anything if you don't," she whispered, trying to remember to smile nicely. The last thing she wanted to do was scare the girl. She had been seen, the only thing she could do now was ensure her departure remained a secret.

"You wanted ice-cream, too?" She lifted the tub from behind her back, extending it towards her. Her beautiful black eyes blinking innocently. "I don't mind sharing, cousin Jesse." Great, Jesse thought, the girl even knew who she was.

"No, I just need some fresh air."

"But it's dark and scary out there," the girl, whispered glancing through the large arched windows. With the lights out, and the freezer door now closed, Jesse could see a brilliant scattering of stars peering down from the night sky.

"No, it's not scary. Come here, let me show you something." She tried the door, locked, just as she suspected it would be. At least now she had an easier way of leaving than searching the house for an open window or a set of keys. "Do you know where the key is?"

"I'm not supposed to open the door at night," the girl replied, dipping her spoon back into the tub.

"You're not supposed to sneak down for ice-cream either, I'll bet. Besides, I want to show you something, you can lock it right back up behind me."

"Okay." The young girl reached into a drawer containing beeswax-coated wrappings and produced the key. With a quick glance behind her to ensure no one was sneaking down to observe her breaking another rule, she slid the key into the lock. Her small fingers fumbled a few times until the key turned, allowing Jesse to open the door. The refreshing nighttime air welcomed her with its cool embrace. There was no other fragrance quite like it. Few things had brought her as much comfort, except for the spicy scent of ginger and cinnamon. Swallowing, Jesse stepped outside on to the wooden decking of the wraparound porch.

"When I was your age, I used to look at the stars all the time with my best friend." Her voice hitched slightly. *No, no time for sadness, just anger,* she reminded herself. Sadness drained the rage, and she needed every simmering molecule. "I was too young to know their names, but I wanted to show off, so I made them up. You see that up there. She pointed out to the sky above the forest, I called that one waving worm. You see how it curls around just a little and its tail looks a little like an open hand."

"No." The girl pouted, squinting at the sky. Jesse huffed a forced laugh. It did seem a little harder to see such things now.

"Well, my point is, all these stars are watching over you, they're working really hard to cast some small amount of light into the world. So, as long as they're there, there's no reason to be afraid of the dark."

"They're really pretty," the girl whispered. "I wish they'd come out in the day when it isn't so scary."

"That's the thing about life, you can't always see the light until real darkness descends."

"What about when it's cloudy?"

"They're still there, you just have to look a little harder sometimes. There's always something lighting your way, even if it's just the freezer door and a midnight snack." She reached out, tapping the girl's nose lightly with an empty smile. Being her friend, playing nice, was the only way to make sure she would keep her word and not tell anyone of her departure.

"Are you sure you should be walking out there at night?"

"With all those stars lighting my way, what could possibly go wrong? Lock the door behind me, okay? And remember, you never saw me, and I certainly didn't see you eating that tub of ice cream."

"Don't you need shoes?" the young girl questioned, pointing at Jesse's socks.

"I don't have any, but I won't be long."

"My sister has some you can borrow, they may be a bit big, her feet are huge." The girl extended her arms wide. "And smelly too."

"Your sister?"

"Freya." Great, that was all she needed. Her only hope now was to put as much distance between them as possible before the young girl told her. Surely she had until morning, by then everything would already be over, by then it wouldn't matter who knew she'd left.

"Sure, I'll borrow some. Hey kid, how old are you?"

"I'm not a baby goat," she said, pouting. "I'm Justine and I'm seven, okay, six and three quarters, but that's almost seven." She opened a small broom closet and pulled out a pair of trainers. "See, told you they were big." The shoes were indeed a good few sizes too large, especially for someone of her own slight frame, but anything was better than nothing.

"Thanks, Justine."

"Cousin Jesse, do you think we could talk more tomorrow? I'd like to hear more about the stars. I think I see it now." She waved her hand towards the night sky, the spoon hanging in her mouth.

"We'll see what happens." Jesse observed the young girl, wondering how long it would be before she too lost her innocence and was forced to grow up. "Now lock the door and off to bed. By the way, if you eat it all, your sister will know for sure someone's been snacking. Always leave a little in the tub."

Jesse stepped from the decking on to the grass, deliberately avoiding the thin gravel path leading towards the rear gate. Like most clan houses, their land was in a place of convenience which allowed them to embrace both sides of their nature.

The estate looked different now that she wasn't fleeing from a wedding or through a window. She cast her gaze to the burning fires in the sky above, a single tear streaking her face. That would be the last one she allowed herself to cry, she swore.

Even after all this time the stars were still so captivating, they could almost make her believe there was still something worth living for beyond revenge. Almost.

Alec sat in his room, his knuckles swollen, oozing with the same fresh blood that streaked the wall where his fists had collided time and time again until he lacked the strength to continue.

He sat now, his fist striking the floor, exhausted. The only small salvation was that Micah had claimed Jesse before her father could complete the rite. But seeing her like that, seeing what his own hands had done to her, he knew the damage had already been done. Her fight had been extinguished. He struck the floor again, his mangled flesh screaming in a protest he ignored.

'Traitor, traitor, traitor.' He pressed the heel of his hand to his heart, his eyes squeezing shut, only to see himself bringing down that weapon again and again. He felt a tug in his chest and was on his feet, staring outside at the night sky before he even knew what had drawn him there. The moon's pale glow illuminated the manicured lawn, turning the grass a beautiful shade of silver. But that was not where his focus was drawn. His gaze locked upon the figure who marched across it towards the path, towards the front door.

No, she couldn't be here. Why the hell would she come back?

He dashed from his room, his hands gripping the door frame as he turned, propelling himself along. She couldn't be here. What was she thinking? His bare feet pounded across the carpet, causing ancient floorboards to creak and groan as he navigated the halls. His heart quickened with every step, beating out its incessant chorus, 'Traitor, traitor, traitor.' He was on the landing when the front doors flew open. Wind howled, blowing her hair wildly as it chased inside, rattling paintings and the ancient wind chimes above the door. She looked like a goddess of fury, and rage burned in her blue eyes with the intensity of a storm.

"Run," Alec croaked, his hand clasping the rail as he began to descend. His words were for her, but they only escaped his lips because he was telling himself to run as much as her. It was the only way he could speak aloud near her. As his panic-stricken gaze met hers, he looked away. He couldn't hold her stare but continued his rapid descent. He had to get her out of here. "Run, now." He had to get her out of here, before...

"Seize her."

'Shit.' The words had been nothing more than a dismissive command, but they plunged his world into chaos once more. He tried to stand fast, stand firm and grip the handrail to prevent his feet from moving. But his gaze had lifted to her and she stared back.

Her eyes which had once held laughter and love now were nothing more than embers of rage. Then he was behind her, tightening his grip as he felt her squirm slightly within his grasp, his fingers digging into her wrists as he held them behind her back. Held them while her father approached. But she didn't fight. She let him restrain her, even though he was certain she knew of at least two ways to break his hold.

"Me for him," she announced defiantly. She jerked her head, flicking her hair behind her shoulder as her gaze locked upon her father. He strode towards her alone, unguarded, down the hallway towards the open front door. Amusement danced in his eyes as he studied the loose nightgown all the way down to the oversized shoes. Something about the way the overhead chandelier cast down its pale light twisted the shadows on his face and made him appear more sinister than normal. He advanced with confidence, but Alec had seen the slightest stiffening of his posture before the slow smile had crept over his face.

"My dear, why would I settle for one when I can have both?" He glanced to Alec.

"Me for him and I won't fight."

"You won't fight me anyway, not if you know what's good for you. One word from me and everyone who followed you here dies." Alec felt her stiffen in his grasp. He could hear his mental pleas as he willed himself to break his orders, *come on, say you're sorry, release her hands, slacken your grip. Do something, anything, don't just stand here. Don't let this happen.* "Oh, you didn't know anyone had followed you? It seems that clan I sold you to wanted more than just your pretty face after all. Do you really think Alec is my only familiar, the only one bound to my service?"

Jesse felt the colour drain from her face. There was only one person who had seen her leave, one person. She was still young, innocent.

She was meant to have locked the door and gone back to bed. She couldn't have followed her here, she wouldn't have, not after all the talk about her being afraid of the dark. Would she?

No, push the worry aside, hold on to the rage, she reminded herself, but it was getting more difficult. She had seen the way Alec had looked at her, she had seen his pain, the way his own soul died slightly as her father's voice commanded him.

There it was, the rage, Alec was suffering, too, because of the monster before her, because of her father. He had lost his life, his freedom, to her father's whims. Her anger was for him, she needed to hold on to it, the way her father was forcing him to hold on to her.

"How do you think your new family will feel suffering at the hands of Burnell? Do you think little Justine will be as strong as you? She's so much younger. What is she, seven, eight? You know, maybe I should have sent him to you when you were her age. I really thought he'd be the one to break you." He stepped forward into the full glow of the chandelier overhead as if entering a spotlight. He extended his arms raising them as if to challenge her to rebel, to test him, to see how far he'd go.

She glanced behind her, but she could only see Alec staring blankly ahead. He had to be bluffing. Surely he only knew of Justine's existence because of the wedding. He would have seen her there, that had to be how he knew her name. She couldn't have followed. It was impossible. She was safe at home in her bed with a stomach full of ice-cream. *Please let her be safe, at home, in her bed.* "I knew you'd come back."

"Me for Alec and Justine. I'll take his place, I'll submit willingly. I'll... I'll bear you an heir with anyone you desire." Did Alec's grip on her wrists just tighten slightly? She wondered as she faced down her father.

"You'd continue our line?"

"If you let them go," she confirmed, keeping the bite in her tone.

"I suppose Burnell does deserve some recognition. Everything he did to you was of his own will, after all. You'd bear his child?" She glared towards her father. *Keep the rage,* she reminded herself as her skin burned remembering his touch. Don't react, don't let him win.

"For their release."

"I never could understand you, pet. Perhaps that's why I could never break you. What I can't grasp is why you would come back, for him of all people." I thought he said he'd knew I'd come back. Her mind raced. Was he bluffing, had her appearance here surprised him? "If he really had any feelings for you, my commands would mean nothing." Jesse felt her heart tearing a little more as her father echoed her own earlier thoughts. Keep the rage. "You can't think any of this make-believe was real. Look at him, he doesn't care about you.

"What good would it do to trade yourself for him? He wouldn't come back to save you, he wouldn't even spare you a second thought." Jesse thought she may have imagined it the first time, but now she was almost certain Alec's grip had tightened a fraction more causing his little fingernail to dig into her skin. "Come now, if you're going to consent, why not let me keep your lover? I could command him to love you again."

The breeze from outside had stilled and her father's syrupy fragrance seemed to coat her mouth, growing stronger with each step he took towards her. "You really have no cards to negotiate with, pet. I have the girl," Alec's fingers dug into her again. She knew it. He was bluffing. It was a sign, it had to be. Alec couldn't release her, he couldn't do anything, except keep her in place. It had to be a message. It just had to be.

If Freya and Micah were correct, if he was fighting in there, fighting to send her a message, causing her pain was not outside her father's command. "I have your new family," another increase in pressure, "and, my pet, I have you." He placed his fingers beneath her chin, lifting her gaze to his. She saw him falter as he realised, too late, his mistake.

"No, *I* have *you*," she snarled. Her eyes gravitated towards his shifter essence. Her rage grew warm within her chest as she extended her aura. She didn't need hands to do what she had in mind, she had only needed him close enough.

His essence swirled within her mental grasp as she snatched his other-self, the bear, forcing its presence into the physical container. Her father cried out, his scream a testament to the agony he endured as she thrust the bear deeper into the vessel until she could see the faintest trace of his human part being pushed aside. It was barely noticeable, a dark outline as the vessel for the essences overflowed.

Fur began to coat his flesh as she mentally delved to snatch the paper-thin fragment of her father, ripping him from the vessel. Her father's body twisted, the bear and human voices screaming briefly in unison to create a haunting sound the likes of which no one had heard before. Her grasp on him remained firm, her anger and rage slowly filtering through her touch as the great bear formed before her.

With an angry cry she forced the power of her rage through her, emptying herself, tearing and stretching her father's flailing spirit, slicing at the very fabric of the connection between man and beast, undoing everything he was. Layer by layer, piece by corrupted piece, she let her rage consume him until everything that had made him, his very essence, became nothing more than motes of energy feeding the power of the universe.

The bear before her roared, slashing out with its enormous claws, its last act of defiance as its knowledge of once being part human began to fade. She felt herself turning, being thrust in a half circle. Her head spun as her vision focused upon the darkness outside, the way the light flooded from the doors to capture the moths, how the distant trees looked black, and how brightly the stars shone despite the light. For a moment, she thought she saw movement from the forest as her chest burned and heart cried out, pulling and tearing as she let go of the last pieces of her rage, the final thing holding her together.

Watch the stars, she told herself, recalling the most beautiful words anyone had ever spoken to her. '*I love you, Jesse Kyron, until the stars burn out and all life fades.*' Her heart beat again, the lights in the sky dimming with the growing ache. Rage had consumed her and now she was empty. There was nothing left, nothing to do but watch the stars fade as she allowed herself to embrace her pain. It was time to sleep.

Something behind her jolted her forwards, a quiet grunt near her ear seemed deafening even though it was no more than a suppressed groan. Alec's hands had slid around her waist, pulling her down beneath him as he fell. The bear behind them, nothing more than beast, roared as Alec shielded her and the creature barrelled from the building.

As she lay pinned beneath him, a sudden surge of power washed over her as she felt her father's legacy transfer to her. The network of familiar bonds now acknowledged her as his heir. Soon they would be free. She was the last with his blood pumping through her veins and soon her heart would surely stop.

Alec fought to find the words he knew he should speak, but he couldn't move, let alone find the strength to whisper. He knew what he wanted to say. He wanted to say that he was sorry, that his life was hers. One more time he wanted to make his declaration of love. To tell her he loved her, and would do so until the stars burned out and all life fades, a truth he had known his entire life.

He wanted these to be the words she remembered him by, but they came out a strangled whisper as he spun her around from the path of the bear's claws. Fire chased across his skin as the animal's powerful claws sliced across his back. His hands slid around her waist, pulling her to the floor. He would shield her with his body. She was the only one for whom he would do this willingly, and, for this moment at least, for the first time he could ever remember, there was no pressure in his mind and his thoughts and actions were entirely his own without a shadow of oppression.

For the next few moments he would do the only thing he had ever wanted to do, protect the woman he loved.

The bear let out a roar, dashing past them through the open door as it became nothing more than an animal, a bear with no memories of anything that came before.

"I'm so sorry, Jess." He felt the tear leak from his eyes as his body grew heavy.

He had always said he'd die for her.

At least was one promise he would keep.

CHAPTER 12

Jesse gasped, dragging herself from beneath Alec's dead weight as something warm penetrated her nightdress, spreading across her skin. She shuddered, the pain in her chest causing explosions of light behind her vision.

She was beyond fatigued. The act of shredding her father's soul had taken everything she had. The gentle wind caused the wind chimes by the door to chime once more as it chased through the house, bringing a coolness to her heated skin. Alec's vision was fixed upon her, his honey coloured eyes glistening with pain and regret while his lips held the barest hint of a smile as he looked upon her.

In that one second, as she saw and felt everything through the familiar bond. Her emptiness, the void left by the burning rage, was filled by something new. Something so overwhelming that her heart, once committed to fail, beat anew.

"Alec," she whispered. The marble entrance hall was cool upon her cheek as she lay looking into his eyes, too exhausted to move. She held on to the connection between them, feeling his pure and genuine love surround her, understanding his pain, his anguish, seeing the torture he had endured at being forced to act against his will, being forced to hurt her. Everything was laid bare for her to see. There were no secrets a familiar could keep from their master.

"I'm sorry," he whispered. "At least I got to protect you once." It was only as she slid her hand across the marble floor towards him she noticed the slow spread of ruby fluid expanding from beneath him. Alarm revitalised her. Adrenaline provided a strength that just moments ago she had lacked.

Pulling herself to her knees, she leaned over him, her eyes misting as she tore the bottom of her nightdress between her teeth, pressing the fabric to the enormous gouges across his back. The thin linen drank the blood greedily as she pressed upon the wounds, trying in vain to staunch the flow.

"No," she whispered, her fingers becoming slick as she pressed harder. "You were meant to live." She tried to swallow a breath as tears leaked from her eyes. "You were meant to live." This couldn't be happening. He was the one meant to walk away from this, not her.

"He needs to shift. It's the only way he's going to survive." Jesse cast a glance towards the door, seeing Micah flanked by Freya and Justine.

"I'm sorry, cousin Jesse. I couldn't get the key to turn. I didn't want to tell, honest I didn't." Justine's voice sounded timid, her small frame hugged against Freya's legs.

"He needs to shift," Freya repeated as Jesse stared blankly at the girl. Her cheeks were soaked with tears, but it seemed to be the result of worry rather than trauma, but her father had been right, someone had followed her after all.

"I told you already, he's not got an animal essence." She saw Levi emerge from behind their legs. He was limping, his quiet cries tugging on her already broken heart. She asked herself how he could have possibly been injured as he came to lie beside her. There was no visible wound upon him, but his pain was apparent. With a slight growl, he lowered his head, resting it upon Alec.

As the faint traces of their auras reacted to their close proximity, she put her hand to her mouth. Levi had never been a guardian spirit.

He was Alec. But that in itself was impossible. Animal essences had to stay close to their vessels, and yet, her eyes beheld the truth. They were two beings, yet also one and the same.

Placing one hand to Levi's spirit form and the other upon Alec, she focused her vision on their aura, desperately seeking any evidence of a bond between them. But if there had been one, it had long been severed. Tears streaked her face as she mentally grasped at their energy, seeking even the slightest scar from their parting, a scar needed to rejoin them. It was tiny, a testament to their years apart, the smallest sliver just above their hearts.

Pulling on the weave in the same way a spinner would, she grasped the tiny scars, stretching and elongating them until they were long enough to be woven together. She had no idea what she was doing, whether this would even work, but every shifter she had seen had been attached to their counterpart by such threads. Tears mingled with her energy as she worked on rejoining the long-frayed and severed bond as she used her fingers to make them whole. To anyone seeing her, she would have looked like a conductor. But instead of directing music, she was guiding energy.

As their soul started to repair, power began to flow through the threads, each one passing through her, triggering images before her gaze.

She saw Alec holding her hand in the gardens. He was almost seven, yet his expression held an age beyond comprehension. With her hand in his, they looked out over the small lake and he swore to her a vow too heavy for any seven-year-old, a vow always to protect her.

It had been that night her father had come for him, dropping him at the base of the very altar she had knelt before, and made him swear his oath. She felt him try to refuse, but he was already bound, already a familiar, and the words tumbled from his lips.

As he spoke, her father invaded his mind, grasping the very core of his being, but instead of trying to find a safe place to retreat, a place away from the pain as she herself had done, he used everything he had, all that he was to seek his other-half and severed the bond between them.

He had not yet turned seven, as such had never known a shift, but he knew where that part of him had slept, and he freed it, splitting his essence and directing it to her, to watch over and protect her. As just a child, he had sought to defend her the only way he could, by destroying an integral part of himself. That had been the day the caracal kitten had first appeared at her side.

Hot tears streamed down her face as she watched her father bind him while the young boy tore apart his soul for her. The single being becoming two, Alec and Levi. But now she was reversing his gift, giving back the part of himself he had lost because of her. By her will, the threads of their once-severed soul rejoined, returning them to one.

Gasping for breath, she pulled away from their energy, her hand resting on Alec's back as her mind sought the only thing her father had given her that she was grateful for, Alec's familiar bond.

"Shift," she whispered.

Yes, mistress.' The reply invaded her thoughts, and, for a moment, the feeling of their link made her dizzy. It wasn't just his reply she felt, but his every anguished thought mingled within his unyielding love. The sensation was overwhelming and all-consuming as everything Alec was once more became hers to observe. She pushed the intrusion aside. His memories were not hers to invade.

The howl escaping him was both man and beast, trapped in an unfamiliar union that was both alien and natural as they tried to understand their bond, how to be one. Levi gently pushed Alec aside, slowly reshaping their vessel. A natural shift was a sight to behold, over in seconds but filled with complexity. A blinding ripple passed over Alec. To anyone other than Jesse it would appear almost as if three successive lightning flashes consumed one form to leave another in its place, but the change was not instantaneous as people believed and she watched in awe.

Flash. The blinding light peeled away, leaving Alec's spirit essence on the floor beside where his body lay with Levi still beside it.

Flash. Waves rippled across the flesh. The energy creating the body changed consistency drawing Levi's spirit towards it like iron filings to a magnet, liquid bones and organs reformed within Levi's image, constructing his skeleton, tendons, muscle, and skin in the shape of the shifter's essence.

Flash. Fur grew, and the spirit took control of the physical form.

This complete reform was why shifting helped to heal injuries, but it wasn't a miracle cure, as the deep gouges still crossing Levi's back displayed. Injuries simply lessened with each shift, speeding the healing, shrinking the wounds as they passed from one form to another. It was magical, otherworldly, but it was no catholicon.

The energy required to complete a shift was tremendous, and the fact an injured shifter possessed only limited strength meant frequent shifting became impossible. Even a healthy shifter usually possessed only the energy for two full circle transformations a day without intervention. The only blessing was the animal essence, usually being smaller, healed at an accelerated rate, but their heart was smaller, weaker, meaning healing time had to be split between the two forms.

"Levi," she whispered, seeing the panting caracal and hearing its soft cries, "Oh, Levi, I'm so sorry, I didn't know, please." She traced her fingers across his fur, stroking him gently, feeling the laboured breathing slow.

How could she have been so blind? Levi had been with her always, sleeping beside her, bringing her comfort. The only other time she had felt that safe was when Alec had held her. She buried her face into his fur, willing him to heal. His chest heaved a deep sigh, remaining depressed, never rising, and her world once determined to repair fractured anew. "No, breathe," The panic in her voice stung her ears. "Come on, breathe."

'I'm sorry, mistress.'

"Breathe."

'I'm sorry.'

"No, come on, breathe for me, Levi, Alec, please. Don't you dare. Don't you dare leave me. Breathe."

"The damage is too severe..." She heard Micah say as his hand fell heavily upon her shoulder with a sympathetic squeeze.

No. "Breathe, damn you." She forced the words through trembling breaths. Her hands were stroking behind his ears, seeking his favourite purr-points, praying for a response.

"Maybe if he'd shifted before today it would have been enough, but the strain of the first shift was too great."

No. "I order you to breathe," she growled, feeling her own breath freezing, becoming harder, becoming trapped by her swelling grief.

"At least they were reunited in the end. They'll find peace."

No. "You can't do this to me. Breathe, damn you!"

"He died protecting you, there's no shame in that. In the end, he showed you his true heart."

"No!" she screamed, knocking his hand away, thrusting her arms wide as her fingers grasped for the very threads of life from the universe around her. There was so much life in this world, so much energy. Why shouldn't she take some? He would not die, not here, not like this. Not because of her. She could not, she would not let him go. He was hers, and he was not allowed to die. But the energy didn't answer her call. It refused to be tamed, to be taken from the things to which it belonged.

'Mistress, I'm sorry.'

"Shut up. I forbid you, you're not allowed to leave me, you hear, never." She felt the familiar bond tying them together begin to weaken. "You're not allowed to leave me. You make this right."

Jesse's eyes blurred, and for the briefest moment she was certain it was caused by the tears she simply couldn't still. She had gone from being consumed with rage to emptiness, only to be flooded with a heartbreak that far surpassed everything that came before. Yes, Alec had hurt her, but so too had he saved her in more ways than he could ever know. Right now, as she looked down upon him and Levi, she was both devastated and livid. How dare he give up, how dare he leave her before making this right, before *she* could make this right.

His whole life he had been her father's puppet, bent to his whim and wishes. She could forgive him. She would forgive him anything, if only he'd come back to her, if he'd just breathe.

He couldn't do this to her, he couldn't hurt her like this. Physical wounds would always fade, but this she couldn't survive. She needed him more than the air in her lungs, than the blood through her veins. Nothing in their past mattered. She needed him, only him.

"You told me until the stars burn out and all life fades," she whispered, "but the stars are still shining." Her voice echoed around her ears and for the first time, she realised Levi's heart hadn't stopped. It didn't sound because the world around her had frozen. The white shades glowed from the marble floor of the hallway, while the pools of blood shone crimson with an intense and quivering aura. Every colour was so vibrant her eyes ached.

She was not beside him, but looking down upon the frozen landscape. Micah's hands were tangled within his hair, a look of distress clearly evident on his face while Freya's hand cupped her mouth, her other arm wrapped around Justine who stood hugging her legs.

Outside, the swirling movement of energy and the spiralling halos of the stars reminded her of the Van Gogh paintings she had once seen in her class before her father had taken her from school. The energy from the world outside had diverted its path, racing towards her outstretched fingers, wrapping itself around her in its powerful embrace.

'What would you be willing to give, little druid?' She stared down at herself, on the tattered remains of her clothes, her dressed wounds and bloodstained skin. There was something primal about the look in her eyes, the way her mouth was frozen in a guttural scream.

For a moment, she wondered if the Jesse frozen in time could see herself looking down upon them. Her hand massaged her ethereal chest, bringing the tether between herself and Alec shimmering to life, connecting both her mortal and ethereal forms with silver threads to his own. She had seen their bond before, and wondered if its presence was what caused her chest to ache so.

Levi lay motionless before her, his reddish-tan coat now matted with blood from the large gashes that looked only a little better than they had upon Alec's back. Beside Levi, almost grey against the vivid colours, lay Alec's ethereal form. He was dying. Their breathing had stopped, their pulse had almost faded. He was meant to live. She would give her life for him to live.

'Anything,' she answered in absolute sincerity. She owed him so much, and not only to make amends for what her father had done to him.

'Anything?' The lilt to the voice suggested something had been wrong with her answer, but if there was, she couldn't see what. It was the truth. There was nothing she wouldn't give. Nothing.

'Yes, anything. My life, my soul, whatever price you can name I'll pay. Just don't let him die. Please, he has to live,' she begged.

'You may regret that promise. Would you care to rethink your answer, anything is never ending in its possibilities.'

'I will have no regrets so long as he lives.'

'You bargain recklessly with things that hold a greater value than you could fathom. But we will help you, this once, but in turn you must do something for us.'

'Anything, name it.'

'There's that word again, do not throw it around so recklessly. Would you really give your all just to save him?'

'My all and more, so much more.' Here, in this strange frozen time, there was a strange detachment to everything she had endured, to her past, to her pain. The only thing able to pierce her was the loss and heartbreak at the thought he would leave this world. Her life for his, her soul for his, whatever they wanted, whatever the price, she would pay without hesitation. She would pay it so he could live, because a world where he didn't draw breath was not one that should be, and it wasn't one she could survive.

'Then, little druid, we have a task for you. This land has always found balance, but now the scales are tipping. War is coming and you will answer. We are awakening the forces of old ready to quell the threat, already one has stirred. Seek her out and help her cause. This blight must be stopped, balance must be restored before it is too late.'

'What of Levi, of Alec?'

'Do we have your vow?'

'As long as they live, yes. I will do whatever you ask of me.' The white threads of life surrounding her physical body, the energy she had grasped for so desperately, became green tendrils of life granting her their use, and time began anew. Her once frozen gaze blinked, her sight still fixed to the place she had once looked down from. She felt the surge of energy, the power of its change. But more overwhelming, the thing that caused her to sob aloud, was the slow, laboured rise of Levi's chest.

CHAPTER 13

Dawn's first light streamed around the edges of the heavy curtains, casting a warm glow in the otherwise darkened room. Small glints of light reflected from the mirror on the far side of the room, bringing Alec's attention to a slumbering figure wrapped in a blanket, and bathed in darkness.

His stomach churned, aware of only snippets of the last few days through fevered sleep and forced shifting. He knew his mind had been drifting in and out of consciousness at first, but he soon realised his times of greatest awareness were when Jesse had been sitting beside him, her hand upon his, or softly stroking his fur.

He closed his eyes. He remembered everything now, about how he had severed an integral part of his soul to protect her when he realised his binding ritual was upon him. Jesse's mother had intended to free him, but instead she had lost her life. She had sacrificed herself to try to ensure he could protect her daughter, but he hadn't, or at least part of him hadn't.

Over the last three days he and Levi had shared a mind, he had shown, through his memories, the suffering she had endured, all of it, and how he would fend off her attackers by mauling their bestial essences to tire the physical body. He saw how Levi had lay with her each night, snuggled close, and the tearing pain of how helpless he had felt at not being able to protect her.

He'd also seen how Levi had growled whenever he'd seen him. How he had frozen on the train platform, recognising him. But he could not attack a physical form. Levi had known Alec was going to hurt her. He had tried to warn her the only way he knew how because he had no human voice, no way to make himself understood, but her heart had held them both in equal adoration, and she'd paid his warnings no heed.

Now he was free from Jesse's father, Levi had accepted his presence and during their reunion their past had become merged. One being, two pasts. The overlap of memories was confusing. He cast a glance down towards his hands, the human hands that had brought her so much pain, hands he couldn't bear to look at.

As if knowing his need, he felt the shift. It was a strange sensation, natural yet unnerving. It felt as if his soul had simply trickled from his body. Then he was Levi, their two minds looking out as one, yet his humanoid form was also standing beside him. It was confusing, disorientating. He was both the caracal and the essence beside him. He wondered if Levi felt the same confusion. He looked towards the figure slumbering in the corner. It would be better he if were gone when she awoke. Though this disorientation was going to take some getting used to.

His footfall was silent as he padded across the wooden floor, squeezing through the ajar bedroom door. He knew it would be better to slip away, to lose himself in the woods and all the scents that beckoned him. He could explore this new side of him, journey endlessly, anything not to have to look upon her again and see the wounds he had caused, and yet the moment his nose caught her scent, his path altered.

He could feel the two parts of him at war, Alec who loved her ferociously but had brought her nothing but destruction, and Levi the part of him who had always been there, comforting her, protecting her, doing everything his human side wished he could have done.

It was Levi who carried them through elongated shadows and shrubbery still damp with morning dew, to sit and watch her.

He could smell her tears, taste her anguish. He had done that to her. Levi's paw hovered uncertainly, the beast also warring within him. A flash of memory assailed Alec, Jesse's hands tracing desperately across his feline body as she pleaded with him not to leave her.

Alec sighed. He had not only broken her spirit, by saving him she had given up her companion, the only being in the world who had never betrayed her. No wonder he couldn't find the balance between himself and his shifter. They were of one being, but of two hearts and minds. They were one, but separate, and both of them loved her.

Now he was outside, Levi withdrew, pulling him into their shared vessel. It seemed he knew words were needed to mend this rift. Moving forward, he emerged from the shelter of the trees. As if sensing him, her head snapped back, her gaze upon him. She was on her feet in an instant, her hand cupped across her mouth as she fled deeper into the garden. *Damn it. She was always meant to run to me, not from me,* he cursed, massaging his chest with the heel of his hand, but he knew he couldn't blame her.

"Jesse, wait," he called, ready to pursue.

"Leave her be, lad." A large man towered above him. Levi recognised him as Micah. "She's got some things she needs to work through before she'll be ready to talk. Back to bed." Alec followed the man, knowing he had no choice. There was only one part of himself that she trusted, one being who had always been there. "I want to sever him," Alec whispered.

"What are you talking about, lad?" Micah asked, closing the door behind them. Alec felt the rough weave of the doormat beneath his damp, bare feet and did his best to dry them before stepping on to the tiled kitchen floor. Freya glanced towards them from the breakfast bar and, collecting her cup of steaming coffee and book, she departed to allow them a moment of privacy.

"Levi. He's the only good thing she's ever known, and she gave him up to save me."

"Think about what you just said there, lad. That should tell you something." Micah leaned back on the grey and white quartz work surface. Alec could feel the intense pressure of his eyes upon him, but couldn't bring his gaze to meet Micah's. Instead, he looked at the damp and muddy footprints he had left tracking across the once clear floor.

"You're a shifter, there has to be a way, a way to undo what she did, right? A way to send him back to her."

"Shifters can't be split from themselves." Micah glanced at his watch, pushing himself up. "I've not seen it done before, you're doing a lot of things to protect her I never thought possible. Now, back to bed. You need rest."

"Some protection," he huffed self-deprecatingly. "Hey, Micah," The man's hand hovered on the door handle, his departure stilled. "Levi's memories showed me you're her uncle. She's going to be safe here, right?" If he knew she was safe, it meant he could leave without regret. She deserved some security, some safety, a place where people would look after her. What she didn't need, was him.

"I won't let any harm come to her."

"Really? Because it sounded to me as if you'd purchased her as a…"

"I'm her uncle. You won't imagine the lengths I went to in the hope of getting her back. She would have been protected and looked after, but she'll not be staying too long." He must have seen Alec's questioning stare because he continued. "Do you remember what she said to her father, the trade she offered?"

"Me for him," Alec repeated, his gaze burning into the tiles.

"She still made that trade for you, only not to her father." Micah turned his back on Alec, ending the conversation as he walked away. He stared after him in disbelief long after the door had closed, wondering what exactly he had meant.

Damn it—Jesse cursed herself. Why had she done that, why had she run? Well, she knew the answer. She was exhausted, she hadn't slept a wink, and now Alec and Levi were more stable, she needed space. She had come here seeking solitude, hoping to find peace within nature's embrace.

The grass whispered, joining in the chorus of the trees as the gentle summer breeze caressed the land. For days she had sat unmoving by his bedside. Seven times since their return had she used her bloodline's hold upon him to force him to shift, and each time he obeyed she felt dirty.

She had simply wanted to command him to wake and, had she done so, he would have obeyed. She hated this. She hated the connection, the control, the thought of all the years her father had used him. The familiar ties let her feel all, know all, access his every thought, his every memory, nothing was private, and she hated what she saw.

She hated how her father would issue commands and send him on missions, how he had ordered him to kill, and how he hadn't even thought to rebel. He simply followed his commands like a good soldier, not even realising he was being controlled.

He still believed the first time he had felt the familiar hold, the hopelessness, had been when he had sought to resist, when he had tried to fight against his master's command and protect her. To him, that had been his first real taste of the bond's power, of what it meant to be owned. He didn't realise everything he had done, every mission he had taken, every task he had completed, had all been the same because at those times he had never sought to resist. He had simply accepted his orders, never even thinking to question them.

She had come outside seeking solitude. The longer she spent with Alec, the more she invaded his mind, seeking each violation of will, each horrific act her father had turned him to. She hadn't eaten or slept for days. She simply sat beside him, hoping to see signs of his recovery so she could sever the bond between them once and for all.

It was needed for now but, as soon as it was possible, it would be destroyed.

No one should have had to suffer as he did, and worse still, he hadn't even realised what was going on. At least she recognised her own abuse. When Freya had entered, insisting she take a moment to gather herself, she had decided a breath of fresh air and a moment apart would help dispel the exhaustion, push away the dreams that played within her mind while she was still awake.

When she had sensed him nearby, she had panicked, not knowing what to say, how to apologise for everything her father had done to him, to his family. She didn't have the words and, selfishly, she missed Levi. For as long as she could remember, the two of them had been together. He had supported her through her darkest times and she had never realised he was a part of Alec.

All those times she had written to him, asking, begging, him to come home, part of him had never left. He had split his soul for her, had always been beside her. She sniffled, then started as she felt the warm brush of fur against her leg.

"Levi," she whispered, dropping to her knees and pressing her forehead to his as her arms wrapped around the large cat. His spirit form felt as soft and real to her as the nights she had spent on the bed beside him, waiting for him to wake. "I missed you, too, but you know you can't keep coming to me now. You're part of Alec, you should be beside him." She buried her head into his fur. Gods, he even smelt like Alec, soft notes of cinnamon and ginger. How had she not realised it sooner? His black tufted ears flicked, and he gave a yawn which turned into the cutest reverberating meow she had ever heard. She lay down beside him, holding him close, savouring the smell of nature, mourning what would be their final goodbye.

When next she opened her eyes, night had fallen. Levi's presence beside her gave some small measure of warmth, but a chill still racked her body. Rubbing her face against him, she smiled at the soothing sound of his purr.

"I miss you, too, but your place is with him now. He's the one who needs you."

'I need you too.' Alec's soft voice caused her to start with the sudden realisation that he was sitting several feet from where she lay, his presence concealed by the very tree she had attempted to scale on her wedding day, but it took her a moment to realise that he hadn't spoken aloud. The voice she had heard was in her mind. He was unaware she knew he was there, or that his every thought was now hers to hear. No wonder her father had known how to hurt her. It wasn't just her he had punished. *'What do I say? Should I even say anything? I'm sorry, doesn't even touch the surface. What I did was unforgivable. Do I try to tell her how hard I fought? No, why would she want to hear my excuses when even I can't stomach to think them? I was weak, I fought for her and failed.*

'Gods, I should have put her on a train the second our paths crossed. Why didn't I? Because I was selfish, I wanted to look after her, to reclaim the part of my soul I had lost and mourned for all those years. Some good that did. I didn't reclaim what I'd lost, I destroyed her. What was I thinking coming here? I should go, so why do I feel the need to stay? To remain beside her, even if only as an outlet for her ire.

'I should leave. But first I need to find a way to sever Levi, he belongs with her, the only part of me that is good belongs with the only good thing that was ever in my life. My light, my Fae. He should be with her and I should go. She would be better off never setting eyes on me again. What was I thinking coming out here? I should be getting as far away from her as possible.'

"Don't," she whispered. She knew he had heard her, but not that she was aware of his presence. She felt him stand, his light footsteps masked in the cool night's breeze. "Please." The warm wind chilled the dampness upon her cheeks she no longer had the strength to wipe away. She felt him freeze, but didn't look back to where he stood. "Don't leave me." She hated how weak she sounded. Levi brushed against her, comforting her trembling body. Her head hung as she heard his footsteps softly recede. "Please, Alec, don't leave me, not again," she whispered into Levi's shoulders as she draped her arms around the spirit.

∼

Alec tiptoed away, her almost silent pleas breaking his heart as she begged Levi to remain with her. Or so he had thought, until he had heard her whisper his name. The sound of her gentle sobs drifted on the wildflower-scented wind as he returned, carrying the only warm thing he could find. Her shoulders shook gently as he carefully draped the long woollen coat around her. Her hands lifted, her fingers almost reaching out to his before pulling the coat around her tightly.

With a slight sigh, he sat down beside her, his shoulder not quite touching hers as he watched her from the corner of his eye.

"I'm sorry for everything. I broke everything that made us work, trust, love, your heart, your soul." His voice wavered slightly. "Words will never be enough to express how truly, deeply sorry I am." He continued staring forward, not daring to look at her in case he lost his nerve to say what he knew must be said. "In olden times, long before the barrier shielded our land, when something was broken they used to use gold to repair it. Because of this, it became something more, something unique and beautiful.

"It didn't matter it had been broken, that it bore scars, because it was loved. Some things take longer to heal, need more time and attention, but, if you'll let me, I'll be your gold. I'll spend the rest of my life pouring my soul into you. You're hurting, and I caused that. I can't take back what I did, I can't make what I did to you, to us, go away, but maybe, one day I can earn your forgiveness, and if you don't want that, then..."

"Oh, Alec." She turned to face him, an intensity in her gaze that almost stopped his aching heart. "We're not broken. We don't need fixing." He was amazed when she didn't recoil as his fingertips brushed away her tears, wiping away her grief if only for the most fleeting moment. "I thought I'd lost you again. You were lying there... there was so much blood." Her head shook softly, her expression one of tormented anguish. "I didn't know what else to do. I had gone to confront him, intending to exchange my life for yours, but there was so much blood, you stopped breathing.

"I-I thought, I thought I'd lost you and it was the worst feeling in the world." She sobbed, pressing her head to his chest, soaking his t-shirt with her tears. He placed a tentative arm around her, and when she still didn't protest against his touch, he pulled her closer, cradling her to him. "I'm so sorry, Alec, can you ever forgive me?"

"Jess, what in all the heavens would I need to forgive you for? I'm the one who—"

"My father enslaved your family, he made you... he... and I didn't know. You were suffering, and I didn't know. Forgive me, forgive me for everything he did to you, for the life you never had because of him, for the things he made you do without you even realising it."

"Jess, I wouldn't trade this life for any other because it brought me back to you." He looked down to her in disbelief. How could she believe, after everything that had happened, that he was the one who had been wronged? Leaning down, his lips brushed against hers, before pulling hesitantly. "I just don't know how to make this right."

"Neither do I. So how about we start like this." Her hand caressed his cheek, scraping against the days of stubble he had yet to remove. She pulled him down, her lips claiming his possessively, hungrily. They kissed with desperation, clinging to one another for life and breath, as their two broken souls melted together, becoming whole as they shared all they were with each other.

CHAPTER 14

*A*lec stood immobilised, his jaw clenched as tightly as his fists. It was raining outside and water streamed across the glass of the sunroom while the rain hammered its own melody on the glass. The sky above was dark, the world outside shimmered with silver streaks of rain that beat the ground with such force that small paw prints appeared in the swelling puddles. This weather reflected his mood perfectly.

"Don't," he pleaded, looking at Jesse with an intensity that made her falter. In her hand she grasped the only katadesmos that had not been broken, the only familiar tie still bound to her. His. "Please, don't."

"We talked about this." The serious draw of her eyebrows caused his heart to quicken. He couldn't believe she was ignoring his wishes, not after everything they had shared. He thought she understood. Yet she had called him here to do the very thing he had asked her not to.

"No, *you* talked. Don't do this. Please don't." He pushed his hand through his brown hair, briefly grasping his long fringe, unable to look at her.

"It's not your choice." She stood before him, staring him down defiantly, daring him to challenge her on this.

"But it should be," he countered. Why was she being so stubborn, did she really not understand? When he was bound to her father there was always an oppressive shadow lingering in the back of his mind. But since his bond had been passed to her he felt light, free. He saw clearly for the first time in his life, he saw his past in a different light and realised how long he had been a puppet. It was different with her.

"Alec, I am not going to negotiate with you. I've made my decision, and that's final." His hand slid in hers before she could prick her finger on the small spike embedded within the lead tablet. The katadesmos were tablets forged of metal, which had been enchanted and carved. They were activated by blood and rites, but could be broken only by the holder of the bond willingly releasing their servant or their bloodline through the use of the small spindle encased within.

"Jess, please don't. I spent ten years wondering if you were dead, fourteen not being able to protect you. Don't you see, if you keep the familiar bond between us I will always be there, even if we are apart. My life for yours."

"No." The firmness in her voice alarmed him. "That was *my* vow, *my* choice. With what I have to do, I don't want to put you at risk. I won't."

"You never elaborated." He knew she had saved him, that her promise had brought him back from the brink of death, but she refused to speak further on the matter.

"I don't understand what is expected myself." He released her hands, waiting for her to continue. "I made a promise in exchange for your life, and I not only intend to fulfil it, but ensure my trade was not in vain." Her thumb pressed down before he had time to move, the lead fractured, before the enchantment within turned the metal in her grasp to putty, then liquid. It dripped through her fingers on to the sunroom floor, pooling and gathering upon the solid surface until a new blank tablet had formed.

Alec felt pain rip through him. It was brief, searing, and all-consuming. He felt as if the blood within his veins had turned to vitriol as the burning fire consumed him. Then, as quickly as it had swelled, the fire died, quenched by her gentle kisses as she erased the tears he didn't realise he'd even shed. Her smouldering gaze fixed him in place just seconds before her mouth gravitated towards his.

Her lips crashed against his, and he answered in kind, drinking in her taste hungrily. She tasted of summer rain and spring flowers. Sweet, tempting, addictive. He knew he would stay in her arms for as long as she would have him. There was nothing he wouldn't do for her, she was his all, his everything, home.

The powerful beat of his heart replaced the sound of the hammering rain. His arm wrapped around the small of her back, pulling her closer as she moaned into his mouth, a sweet delicate sound that caused his loins to burn. He trailed his kisses down her neck, growling as she wrapped her legs around him, clinging on to him desperately as his lips sought her mouth once more.

He would never tire of kissing her, he would never let her go again. He had spent fourteen years trying to get home, and now she was beside him he would do everything within his power to keep her safe.

A metal perimeter encompassed the land before them. The matt barbed wire and galvanised steel seemed to absorb the sunlight that streamed through the broken clouds above. It was a daunting boundary with chain-link wire creating a secondary barricade fixed tightly against the large steel fences that were curled in barbed wire, top to bottom, before wrapping like a concertina around the top. But Jesse was not looking at that barrier, it was the third protection which caused her pulse to race. An orb of iridescent magic shimmered, unseen to all eyes but her own.

Before them, the wide road they had walked disappeared behind a large sliding gate. She knew, without a doubt, the two guards stationed at the gatehouse were aware of their arrival. She stood frozen, her stomach contracting as she stared ahead of her. Alec squeezed her hand, turning her into his embrace to place a delicate kiss on her lips, tearing her vision from the daunting area before her with the best distraction possible.

"Alec, are you sure this is what you want?" Jesse questioned, staring down at their interlaced fingers instead of at the large, foreboding metal gates before them. She had abolished the familiar bond with him, but still she felt his presence. If anything, the link between them was stronger than before, but his thoughts were his own, his will never to be influenced again, and yet somehow she felt everything.

"I never want to be away from you again, not for one second." He raised her hand to his lips, brushing a kiss across each of her fingers in turn. "Besides, I'm more than qualified."

"You never really told me about your school." She had pried into his thoughts, but only looked at her father's influence, what her father had forced him to do through the familiar bond. Everything else, no matter how tempting it had been, she had left private. His life was his, and if he wished to share any part of it with her, he would.

"It was a military institution. Your father wanted me trained in combat."

"That explains it," she whispered, a blush creeping over her cheeks.

"What?"

"When we first reunited, you were barking orders at me."

"I was?" His chuckle made her toes curl. She could never tire of hearing him laugh, or seeing the way his honey eyes sparked with amusement.

"You most certainly were." His laughter soothed her frayed

nerves, and all too soon she found her gaze peeling away from him to focus once more on the monstrous gates.

"So are you finished procrastinating?"

"No, not yet. What rank were you?" She bit her lip.

"Captain."

"Captain Hayes," she whispered breathlessly, pressing herself against him. She heard him growl as her lips pressed to his. "Now that's about the sexiest thing I've ever heard. O Captain, my Captain." She kissed him again and, moving to stand beside him, she grasped his arm, draping it around her shoulder as she committed herself to the approach. He held her close, his spicy scent calming her nerves.

"You know I have no intention of dying again, right?" he whispered, teasing a smile from her. "I'm going to stay right here, by your side, forever."

Just as they were about to announce themselves, a dark vehicle pulled up outside the gates. A fair-haired man emerged from the driver's side, strolling to the gates with such perfect timing he arrived at the partition just as they did. Jesse took a brief moment to study him. He was not a shifter, and yet he was more than just human.

She saw the shimmer of ice within his aura, the song of a bird within his single soul. It took a second for her to realise what he must be, an ice elemental. He wore the standard P.T.F. issue tactical gear that was night-sky dark, with their emblem embroidered on the front right pocket that was just peeping from beneath his dark jacket. The combat trousers fit his sculpted form perfectly, but she wondered how many people who gazed upon him would see how magnificent he truly looked in uniform.

"Miss Kyron, Captain Hayes, welcome to P.T.F. Headquarters. We've been expecting you." His amiable smile was disarming, friendly, not at all what she had expected. The mechanical gates buzzed and whirled before smoothly sliding apart, granting them entry.

"Expecting us?" Alec questioned, positioning himself so his

shoulder was just slightly in front of Jesse. She placed a reassuring hand on his arm.

"Yes indeed. I am P.T.F. alpha Alex Ciele." He tapped his jacket, bringing their attention to his rank. He opened the vehicle's rear door, and she hated that she flinched as his hand touched her arm to help guide her inside.

"Your glamour is flawless," Jesse announced as he slid into the driver's seat. He glanced at her through the rear-view mirror.

"That should be something kept between ourselves." His voice was serious, friendly yet stern, as his eyes met hers through the mirror.

"What glamour?" Alec whispered, Jesse looked to him and shrugged.

"I am not often this side of the barrier, my forte is undercover infiltration. For security purposes, no one here knows what I actually look like, and I look different to everyone, even the members of my own team. When I am on mission, it conforms to a specific look," he explained, despite there being no need for him to offer further information.

"Is it the frost bird that makes it so seamless?" Jesse queried. She saw him smile and wished she could read his mind. There was something to that look she couldn't decipher. He seemed almost impressed.

"Yes, my aura is flooded with small ice particles that alter light, perception, and people's memories of me ensure I look the same to them as when last they saw me. So, Jesse Kyron, what exactly is your forte?"

"I thought you said you were expecting us," Alec commented, shuffling to make himself more comfortable on the expensive leather upholstery.

"Oh, we were. Jack, our soon-to-be resident psychic, made it very clear you were coming and were to be welcomed. What he couldn't see is what you do."

"No one can see what I do. I-I see nature spirits, including other essences. The dryads sent me to you," she explained through a difficult swallow. Her muscles tensed as the fingers twisted her seatbelt to avoid meeting his eyes again as they flicked back from the road towards her.

Her breathing began to tremble. The warmth of Alec's hand on top of her own brought a rush of comfort. He leaned in, whispering softly in her ear, reassuring her she was safe, as if he knew the dark turn her mind had taken, as if he too felt the imaginary flogger bearing down, punishing her for lying, for her insanity.

Alex didn't speak, but she could feel him watching, no doubt wondering why an admission of her gift would almost bring on a panic attack. When her breathing calmed once more, and she found the strength to lift her gaze, only then did he respond.

"I was curious what would drive you to our gates." As simple as that. No questioning her, no look of disbelief, just acceptance. Alec squeezed her hand again. She gave him a small nod, reassuring him she was all right.

"I can also control them," she added, now the overwhelming pressure in her chest had relented.

"The nature spirits?"

"No, maybe, I don't know, but I can manipulate the other essences. I also see magic, like the barrier you have surrounding this encampment." As she spoke, she saw Alex nodding his head in subtle approval. "So you knew we were coming, but why would you want us?" She knew the P.T.F. were very particular about who was welcomed into their ranks. She had half expected to be turned away at the gates.

"We're assembling a unit geared towards uncovering the source of Pyrexia Blight. We've been following Capitan Hayes's movements for years, but his status as a familiar meant we couldn't risk approaching and tipping our hand." She felt herself straighten. How was it possible so many people knew he was a familiar? It almost seemed as if everyone knew but her, which had to be impossible. A familiar could never disclose their servitude.

"And you can now?"

"Well, he's come to us now, and we heard about your father's death, how you broke all familiar ties he had in place. You've actually already dealt a huge blow to the movement just by doing that. If Captain Hayes agrees to attend a debriefing, we can arrange a transfer of his credentials into our service while we get your training under way."

"Training?" Jesse echoed uncertainly.

"This new unit is only in its development phase and, apparently, still incomplete. It is comprised of civilians with no experience. Our first priority will be to ensure you're all capable. Meanwhile, our investigations continue."

LETTERS SHARED

YEAR 1 (11 & 14)

Alec,

Dad took away my device, but I managed to get the address you're staying at from Martha. You remember her, right? The maid who father assigned to me when he thought it was inappropriate for you to attend to me any longer. She's going to get this to you, and if you write back, she'll get it to me. Please write back, I miss you.

Fae

Fae,

Why did he do that? Are you doing okay? It's strange here. The work is hard. I'm not sure how much you know about where I am, but I'm not meant to say anything so I won't in case they stop my letters. I'm exhausted most days, but I'm getting stronger. When I come back I will definitely be able to protect you. I'm going to work hard for you, Fae. You'll see.

A

Alec,

I'm so glad you wrote back. It's so lonely here without you.
Fae

Fae,

What about your school friends? How are they doing?

There are loads of people here, but the nights are quiet and I can still see the sky. I still smile when I think about naming the stars with you. Even if we're apart, we'll always have the stars, right?
A

Alec,

You're right. I like to close my eyes and pretend we are looking at them together.

Last night, waving worm made an appearance through the clouds just long enough to make me smile. Honestly, how could you not have seen it as that? It's clearly a worm with a hand on its tail.
Fae

YEAR 2 (12 & 15)

Fae,

Sorry it took me so long to write back.

Training here is brutal. But I push past the pain for you. I am getting stronger and when I come back I'll protect you for sure.

Waving worm, honestly, that's almost as bad as you naming Hercules Earthworm Jim. Yes, okay, I see it, the super-suit and everything but come on, no one but us will even get the reference. But that's what makes it so special. What is your obsession with worms? You never did tell me.
Alec

Alec,

Please don't push yourself too hard.

Fae

Fae,

Is everything okay? I got the strangest feeling something was off, maybe because I'm getting used to more than just a few words from you.

You should have seen me yesterday, I beat my best time on the obstacle course. I hold the record now.

A

Alec,

Yes, sorry. I was just pining for you. Pathetic, I know, but it seems like so long since I last saw you.

Great job on your time, I bet all the girls there are fawning over you.

To answer your other question, I don't have an obsession with worms. There just happens to be two in the sky, and don't forget, the great Earthworm Jim has to defend the naïve and innocent Waving Worm from the four seagulls. If he wasn't there, what would happen then, hmm?

My heart is aching with the need to see you. Are you coming home soon? Do they even have school holidays there?

Fae

Fae,

Haha, yes then the four seagulls merge and become Fat Bird, right? That's what you said the night you couldn't see Jim.

No, no school holidays. Did you see outside last night? The heavens were aflame with shooting stars. I know I shouldn't tell you what I wished for, but I wished that you were happy. Are you happy?

A

Alec,

How many times do I have to tell you, they're not shooting stars. It's battle. It looked like Stick Man won this round, though.

What kind of school has no holidays?

Fae

Fae,

This one, but you didn't answer my question. Are you happy?

Stick Man, really? Because from where I was, it seemed like he was down.

A

Alec,

He wasn't down, he was shooting from the ground, it's called tactics.

Hey, it's snowing here. It made me remember the time we had that huge snowball fight. Do you remember?

Fae

Fae,

Of course I remember, we had to dry off before we got back to yours because you were worried your father would be angry.

Speaking of your father, is everything okay at home?

Alec

Alec,

I miss you more each day.

Come home.

Fae

YEAR 3 (13 & 16)

Fae,

I'm getting worried, that's the second letter with blood on it. Don't try telling me it was ketchup, I know blood when I see it.

What's going on?
Alec

Alec,
Oops, sorry. My face is burning now. Just a nosebleed. I'm getting a few of them lately. It's nothing. Hormones maybe.

So tell me about your school. Have you got friends, a girlfriend?
Fae

Fae,
You know there's no one else for me. No one my heart yearns for. I wanted to say this in person but I feel you need to know, I love you, Jesse Kyron. I'll love you until the stars burn out and all life fades.

There's no one for me but you.
A

Alec,
I love you, too. My memories of you are what keep me going.

I'm going to come and visit you. Don't tell anyone, okay? I'm going to ~~escape~~ sneak out.

If everything goes to plan I'll be near your school next month. I just need to wait for the right opportunity. The last Friday of the month, can you get out and find me? It's your birthday, I want to give you something.
Fae

Fae,
Escape? Why would you need to escape? Yes, I could see what you wrote through your crossings-out.

I'll be there. No matter what, I will always find you.

I can't wait.
A

Fae,

You didn't show. Is everything okay? I waited all night. What happened? Talk to me.

A

Alec,

Sorry I made you worry. Father caught me trying to sneak out the window.

He's had it bricked closed now, there's only the slightest opening. I can hardly see the stars anymore.

Alec, I miss you.

I'm so sorry I ruined your birthday. Did you have a good time?

Fae

Fae,

He's bricked your window closed? Why were you climbing out your bedroom window? You could have broken your neck.

Jesse, I'm getting worried, what aren't you telling me?

A

Alec,

It was my own fault. I keep making him angry. You know he has a temper.

Fae

YEAR 4 (14 & 17)

Fae,

It's not your fault, Jesse, it's never your fault. Don't let him do to you what he did to your mother.

Please, Jesse, tell someone. The blood on your notes, they're not from nosebleeds are they? He's hurting you, isn't he? He's hurting you and I'm trapped here. I'm getting stronger, Jessie. I'm coming back for you, don't ever forget that.

I'm coming back for you.

A

Alec,
I hold on to that every day. You said you're trapped there. Is there something you're not telling me?
Fae

Fae,
Why are you writing with your left hand, I can tell from the scrawl before you say you're not.
A

Alec,
Just trying something new. I read that people who are ambidextrous use more of their brains.
Did you see the stars last night? Even through my slit of a window, they looked amazing. I hope you were seeing them too.
Fae

Fae,
I look for them every night so I can feel closer to you. I think about the nights we spent in the garden on the picnic blanket once the house lights were out. Do you still go there?
A

Alec,
Oh, Alec, I miss you so much. I wish you were here, I wish I was in your arms. Your letters smell like you, did you know that? It smells like home. I keep them hidden in the vent so I can breathe you in when it feels like I'm suffocating.
My heart is hurting for you. When are you coming home?
Fae

Fae,

I have some things I need to tell you about this school, but it's not the kind of thing I can do in a letter. I will explain everything when I come home to you.

Wait for me, okay?

A

Alec,

I would wait until the end of time. You know I love you.

Fae

Fae,

This is so hard. I wish I was there holding you. I miss the smell of your hair, the sunshine in your smile. I miss being home in your arms.

This time apart is killing me. But I am getting stronger, week by week, month by month.

Soon I will be strong enough to keep you safe. Wait for me a little longer. I love you so much. I think about you all the time.

A

Alec,

I'm scared. Please come home. I've been lying. Things here aren't okay. They haven't been okay since you left, and not just because you're not here.

I thought I could handle it. I was wrong. It's getting worse. When it was just his fists that was one thing, I could numb the pain, I got used to it. But last night he was like a man possessed. I've never seen such rage. He used his belt on me, Alec. He beat me until I blacked out, until I bled.

I thought he was going to kill me. You're right, I should have told someone, but I'm a prisoner. I can't do this anymore. Please come for me. I can't do this anymore. I need you. I really need you. I don't think I can survive this. Please, Alec, I need help.

Fae

LOST LETTERS TO ALEC

YEAR 5 (15)

Alec,

I'm sorry. I shouldn't have written that last letter to you. I haven't heard from you in weeks. Please forget I said anything. I'm sorry, please write back.

Fae

Alec,

Do you still look at the stars? I told you father sealed my window, didn't I? But there's still a small space. I can still see our constellations. I wonder if you look at them too. I like to think you do, that you still think of me. Why haven't you written back?

Fae

Alec,

Do you think I blame you for what happened? Because I don't. I never could. I know you have your reasons, I know you are trying, I feel it in every letter you write. You love me and, if you could, I know you would be here. I don't blame you. I miss you. I miss my best friend.

Fae

Alec,

This silence is deafening. Whatever I did to make you stop writing I'm sorry. I need you, I love you. Please don't forget me, forgive me.

Fae

YEAR 6 (16)

Alec,

I need you, Please I just... I need you, I need your strength.

I feel so dirty, I need you to tell me it's okay, tell me something, anything.

I turned sixteen today.

I wanted you to be my first but he's even taken that from me now. But you will always be my first love.

Please come home. I need you to hold me.

Fae

Alec,

I haven't seen the stars for weeks. I wonder if you can see them where you are.

Fae

Alec,

I hate you, really, I mean it, I. Hate. You. How could you leave me here? You promised to protect me.

I was lying before. I do blame you. If you had kept your promise, I wouldn't be here now. It's not just a belt anymore, but what do you care? You left me here. You really left me here. How could you forget me so easily when you consume my every thought?

I hate you, Alec. I really fucking hate you.

Jesse, because I'm clearly not your Fae anymore.

YEAR 7 (17)

Alec,

I'm sorry, I don't hate you. I love you. I love you so much it hurts and it's killing me how much I need you. It's killing me you're not here, that you think I'm so damaged that you can't even bring yourself to write to me.

I wish I could take it all back. I wish I'd never told you.

Can we pretend I never told you?

Jesse

Alec,

Do you remember when you first called me Fae? You said it was because I was always busy making mischief. I wish for those simpler days. I don't feel like that young girl anymore.

Jesse

Alec,

All the scent has gone from your letters now. I'm not really sure when it happened, but I noticed it, or maybe noticed again today. Sometimes it's hard to remember what you smell like.

Can you maybe write me just once? Just one letter so I have something other than the smell of lavender and beeswax. I hate this smell. It makes me sick.

Jesse

Alec,

Whatever I did to make you forget me, I'm sorry.

I don't need anything from you, just let me know you're still out there somewhere, let me know you're happy. One of us should be. Please tell me you're happy.

Jesse

YEAR 8 (18)

Alec,

Are you getting my letters? Martha says you are, so why aren't you answering?

He's hurting me, Alec. Worse than ever before. I may not have you in body or soul any more but I have you in mind. My thoughts of you are all that keep me going. I still run to your arms when I am scared, but now they exist only in my mind.

One day, I hope you will come back to me. I guess I'm just being foolish.

Jesse

Alec,

You must think I'm pathetic, still writing to you when you've made it clear you don't want to know. It's just I can't let you go. You're my heart.

Jesse

YEAR 9 (19)

Alec,

I'm sorry I didn't write for a while. I know you're still getting my letters, maybe you read them, maybe you don't and if you don't, perhaps one day you will and will take pity on me and just write one final letter.

Things are getting bad, but I've endured worse, like this silence. It's killing me, Alec.

Are you still out there?

Jesse

Alec,

I need help, Alec, if you ever felt anything for me, please report him. I need help, he's going to kill me one of these days.

Please, Alec, no one here even cares when I scream.

Jesse

Alec,

You know what. I'm done.

While you're out there living, screwing, being happy, I am stuck here enduring his touch. The sick thing is, I don't even mean my father. Some days I would rather his beatings to what he lets Burnell do to me.

Think of that next time you're fucking your girlfriend, think of his hand covering my mouth, suffocating me while he drives himself into me repeatedly. As your girlfriend cries out, imagine my screams.

Think of me, I dare you.

Jesse

Alec,

I want to stop writing. I'm so angry at you. You've abandoned me. I really am all alone. I'm so fucking angry at you right now. I'm angry but... forget it, what do you care?

Jesse

Alec,

I'm sorry. I'm so sorry. I really do hope you have a girlfriend. I hope she makes you happy.

Please just forget my last two letters. It's been hard. Last month, I nearly died. He beat me until I passed out, I couldn't breathe, I couldn't even get out of bed. I thought I was stronger. It's not your fault, none of this is. I was angry but not at you, never at you.

Jesse

YEAR 10 (20)

Alec,

I want to stop writing, to give you peace from me. But I'm sorry, the hope of you responding one day is sometimes all I have. The thought of at least someone out there knowing what is happening brings me comfort, even if you can't bring yourself to reply, at least you know.

I miss you. Our favourite constellation is here again, are you seeing it, too? Do you still think of me?

Jesse

Alec,

I don't know what to say but I needed to write. I've been thinking a lot about the past. Do you still remember how we used to walk to the cafe after school? We'd share ice-cream or cakes. I can still remember how much better things tasted when I was with you.

Jesse

Alec,

You're really not coming back for me, are you? I don't think you'd recognise me anymore anyway, so maybe it's just as well. I don't even know who I am.

I don't blame you for moving on, I just wish you'd told me because I still hold on to the childish hope you'll write back.

Jesse

YEAR 11 (21)

Alec,

I turned twenty-one today. Do you remember when I turned four, and we blew the candle out on the cake my mum made? It was more spit than icing by the time we'd done, but we still ate it anyway. It's one of the only good memories I have left of her.

I miss you.
Jesse

Alec,

I hate you. I hate you for leaving me here, for forgetting me while you get on with your life. I hope you're as miserable as I am.

Jesse

Alec,

I'm sorry. I don't hate you. I've never hated you. I love you. Please write back. Let me know you're happy. I want to know you're happy.

Jesse

Alec,

I'm so tired. I don't think I can fight any more. It's easier when I just accept my fate.

Jesse

Alec,

Fuck you. I can't keep doing this to myself. You've forgotten me, I'll forget you, too.

Goodbye, Alec.

Jesse

YEAR 12 (22)

No letters

YEAR 13 (23)

No letters

YEAR 14 (24/25)

Alec,

I'm sorry. Whatever I did, whatever I said, I'm sorry.

This really will be my last letter. Father sold me. I'm getting married a week on Saturday. I'm scared, Alec. No good will come of this.

Please, I will never ask anything of you again, I'll disappear and leave you to whatever life you have, but please, please come for me. Please don't abandon me.

Jesse

LOST LETTERS TO JESSE

YEAR 5 (AGE 18)

Jesse,

Please hold on. I'm coming. I have a plan. Please tell me you're alright. If all goes well, you'll be in my arms tomorrow night. You should have told me sooner.

A

Jesse

I'm so sorry. They caught me trying to leave. I've been in solitary, but it just meant I had time to think of another plan. I'm not giving up.

Please let me know you're okay.

A

Jesse

Why have you stopped writing? Is it because I didn't come? I promise I am trying. I will find a way to you. I promise.

A

Jesse,

I love you. I need you to know that. I need to know you're safe, please just one letter.

A

Jesse,

Okay, I lied too. I lied when I said this was a school, it's not, it's a prison. No one ever leaves, not until their employer sends for them. Your father sent me here so I can learn to serve him, but it isn't him my soul wants, it's you, always you. That's why I need you to know I will come for you. It's just not easy.

I need to know you're safe, please.

A

YEAR 6 (19)

Jesse,

The stars were so bright tonight. I sat all night until dawn imagining I was with you.

Do you still look at them, too? Do you still think of me?

A

Jesse,

Happy sweet sixteen. I haven't forgotten my promise. Even if you spit in my face and send me away, I am still coming, at least then I will see you, know you are safe, alive. I just haven't found a way yet. Gods know I'm trying. I haven't forgotten you. I could never forget you.

Have you forgotten me? You are alive, aren't you?

A

Jesse,

I have a girlfriend. Her name's Sam. I've moved on, now will you please just let me know you're safe. Just one moment of your time.

If you want to leave me in the past that's fine, I understand. I've moved on, too.

Please let me know you're safe, let me know you're happy.

A

Jesse,

Still nothing? I broke things off with Sam. She was a great girl but you know what, she wasn't you. No one will ever be you.

A

Jesse,

I have a horrible feeling something terrible has happened. I can't shake it. I keep hearing you cry in my dreams. This is breaking my heart. Please, please just let me know you're okay.

A

YEAR 7 (20)

Jesse,

What the hell? I wrote to your school thinking maybe you would answer if I wrote to you there. They said you haven't been there since I left. Why didn't you tell me? What's going on?

I keep rereading your letters, he's keeping you prisoner, isn't he? He has to be. He took your device, blocked your window. Why didn't I see it?

A

Jesse,

Am I just being paranoid thinking you're a hostage? Have you moved on? If you have, just tell me. Otherwise know that I am coming for you, I don't know how, or when, but I am coming.

A

Jesse,

Tonight's the night, be ready.
A

YEAR 8 (21)

Jesse,

I almost made it. Shit, I was so close.

I'm sorry. I won't stop trying to get to you. Do you hear that? Unless you tell me otherwise, I'm going to keep trying to get to you.

A

YEAR 9 (22)

Jesse,

I found a way out. It's not ideal, in fact, it's a long way from ideal. Apparently if I make captain, they have to discharge me. Escape is out of the question, the perimeter is too secure. I found out it's not only fencing and guards but magic. I couldn't leave, even if I found a way past the barricade. I feel truly helpless so I will do the only thing I can. I'll work hard.

A

Jesse,

Please let me know you're okay. I keep looking at the last letter you sent. I keep rereading it. Is he still hurting you, is that why you can't write back?

You are alive, aren't you? Please tell me you're still alive.

A

Jesse,

I can't keep doing this. I don't know if you're okay but I'm not. This is killing me. Are you angry because I wasn't there? Is this your way of punishing me for breaking my promise? I'm sorry, okay? Is that what you need to hear? I am so sorry.

A

Jesse

I was sent on my first mission this week. I saw someone who looked a little bit like you. Was it you? Is that why you're not answering, because my letters aren't reaching you? Who am I kidding, I know it wasn't you. My heart knows you without compromise.

A

YEAR 10 (23)

Jesse,

I'm sorry if you're trying to let go. If my letters remind you of the past. Write to me, tell me to stop, tell me you hate me, that you're angry. Anything. Just don't shut me out like this.

A

Jesse,

You didn't write, so I'm going to keep trying. You know I love you. I will forever, always, until the stars burn out and all life fades.

Always, Jesse, no matter what.

Please tell me what's going on. What can I do? How can I make you forgive me?

A

Jesse,

I keep trying to let you go. It's clearly what you want. But I can't. I feel like I'm not complete, like I am missing part of my soul. You complete me, Jesse Kyron. Anyone else is just a poor substitute.

A

Jesse,

Even though you don't reply, I hope you are getting these letters. I hope one day you will forgive me.

I broke my promise, he hurt you, and I couldn't protect you. I couldn't even get away from this place. I know you must hate me, but know that I hate myself more.

You're the one person I never wanted to let down. The most important person in my world, the breath in my lungs.

Without you, I feel like I'm slowly dying. I just need to know you're okay.

A

Jesse,

I look at the stars every chance I get. I try to find a way to bridge the distance between us, to connect our hearts and souls. But I guess I am the only one reaching.

At least I have you in my dreams.

A

YEAR 11 (24)

Jesse,

Did you know I dream about you? I have done for a long time. We're in a cottage together, holding each other as we gaze out at the stars. I want to hold you like that for real.

A

Jesse,

I keep telling myself I should stop writing, that I should let you go. But then I worry, what if you still read my letters, what if they help you somehow with whatever you are going through? But if that's the case, why won't you reply?

A

YEAR 12 (25)

Jesse,

    I kissed someone today. I've been trying to move on again. But no matter what, no one has ever held a candle to you. No one. Do you remember our first kiss? That butterfly-light kiss. Nothing has ever compared to that.

    A

Jesse,

    It's been a bad year for me, and not just because I don't know what happened to you. Things are getting harder. I thought I could get through this for you, in the hope your father will one day allow me back.

    I didn't tell you this, but it's only fair you know—actually, never mind, if you want to know, ask me.

    Please, ask me.

    A

YEAR 13 (26)

Jesse

    I can't shake the feeling something is wrong. I've been dreaming about us in that cottage a lot. I keep thinking it's your way of reaching out to me. Are we sharing dreams or am I the only one who's dreaming?

    A

Jesse,

    I bet we've both changed so much. You probably wouldn't recognise me now, but I would know you in a blink. I got my final promotion, it means my training here is nearly at an end.

    Should I still come for you? My soul cries for you, but my mind is conflicted.

If you needed me, you'd have written back, right? What should I do? Tell me what to do.
A

Jesse,

Please, Jesse, just write to me, sign your name on a blank paper, anything so I know you're okay.
A

Jesse,

You must hate me. I'm sorry I failed you. I wish I could have been there for you. I wish I could have kept my promises, but sometimes even the greatest wishes fall shy.
A

YEAR 14 (27/28)

Jesse,

I'm coming home. Finally. I'm being sent back to you.

I'm getting you out of there. Just wait a little longer. I know it's unfair of me to ask. I've kept you waiting so long. Just a little longer, okay?
A

Jesse,

What the hell, Jesse, you're getting married and didn't think to tell me? I saw the announcement. This is why you've been ignoring me, isn't it? Obviously, you had no trouble moving on.
A

Jesse,

Why didn't you tell me yourself about your wedding? Is it because you're still angry, because I failed you? I tried, I really did. Maybe one day I can explain, maybe one day you'll forgive me.

A

Jesse,

I'm writing this on the train. I'm going to find you and place this in your hand, and if you still don't answer me, if you still can't reply, then I guess there's nothing left for us to say.

All these years, I held on to the hope you were safe. I awaited a reply that never came and it killed me not knowing if you were alive.

By the time I arrive, you'll already be married. I truly hope you're happy. Are you?

I've made mistakes, I've done things I'm not proud of, things that can never be forgiven, but I love you and that's the one thing I have never regretted. You've always been the one for me, I know this, it's always been you. Only you.

I love you, Jesse Kyron, I always have, I always will, until the stars burn out and all life fades.

I know you don't feel the same, but can you find a way, some way, no matter how small, to keep me in your life since we'll be living in the same town? It would kill me if I had to see you, and you acted as if we were strangers. I know I failed you, that you owe me nothing, but can you find it in your heart to find even the smallest corner of your life for me?

Yours always,

A

Dear reader,

We hope you enjoyed reading *Familiar Ties*. Please take a moment to leave a review, even if it's a short one. Your opinion is important to us.

Discover more books by Kathryn Jayne at

https://www.nextchapter.pub/authors/kathryn-jayne

Want to know when one of our books is free or discounted? Join the newsletter at

http://eepurl.com/bqqB3H

Best regards,

Kathryn Jayne and the Next Chapter Team

Lightning Source UK Ltd.
Milton Keynes UK
UKHW011838080121
376714UK00001B/87